"Are you ticklish?"

Suddenly Eva stopped laughing and gasped again, looking down at her struggling body beside Adam's. The loosened swimsuit had been worked downward until her small, high breasts were almost exposed. Adam looked, too. His clear brown eyes rose to hers, and Eva recognized a light she'd seen there twice before.

Adam let go of her wrist and slowly brought his hand to her heaving chest. Eva grabbed his wrist with the intention of stopping him. But Adam was already slowly lowering her swimsuit.

Her other arm was under him, and Eva couldn't move. But in that moment, she didn't really think to. For days, she had felt a strange uneasiness that she was reluctant to acknowledge. It was there again, and she recognized it as a desire for Adam to touch and hold her....

Sandra Kitt

Adam
and *Eva*

Published by Silhouette Books
America's Publisher of Contemporary Romance

SILHOUETTE BOOKS

ISBN 0-373-28557-4

ADAM AND EVA

Copyright © 1984 by Sandra Kitt

This edition published by arrangement with Harlequin Books S.A.

® and TM are trademarks of Harlequin Books S.A., used under license.
Trademarks indicated with ® are registered in the United States Patent
and Trademark Office, the Canadian Trade Marks Office and in other
countries.

Visit Silhouette Books at www.eHarlequin.com

Printed in U.S.A.

SANDRA KITT

has appeared several times on the Black Board bestseller list in *Essence* magazine and was nominated for the prestigious NAACP Image Award for Fiction in 1999. She was also the recipient of its Lifetime Achievement Award from *Romantic Times Bookclub,* and was presented with the 2002 Service Award from Romance Writers of America.

A native of New York, Sandra holds a bachelor and master's degree in fine arts, and has studied and lived in Mexico. A one-time graphic designer and freelance illustrator, she has exhibited across the U.S. and is in several corporate art collections, as well as the Museum of African American Art in L.A. She has designed cards for UNICEF and illustrated two books for the late science writer, Dr. Isaac Asimov. A frequent guest speaker, Sandra has lectured at NYU, Penn State, Sarah Lawrence and Columbia University, and teaches courses on publishing and fiction writing. She has appeared on *Today NBC, Black Entertainment Television* and *Good Morning, America.*

Chapter One

The plane dipped again, and Eva felt her stomach lurch upward into her rib cage, pressing uncomfortably in her mild panic. Her hands gripped the armrests with such force that color began to drain from her knuckles. Her well-shaped head with its short crop of gently layered curls was also pressed with equal force into the headrest. Anyone looking at Eva Duncan in that moment would have suspected that the woman was merely waiting out the boring process of the landing of the Boeing 727 jet. They would not have seen the distress that held her prisoner and which, in fact, held most people prisoners on their very first plane flight.

Eva completely missed the developing panorama out the window of the Caribbean Sea, spotted with islands of varying size and topographic details. She missed the aerial view of dozens of white-sailed vessels gliding along the aqua surface of the water below. But she also missed the plane touching down on the St. Thomas runway, looking for all the world as though it were headed for the mountains in front of it.

"We're on the ground," came the knowledgeable child's voice next to her. Eva opened her eyes and turned to look into the calm, wide-eyed face of her flight companion.

"You can open your eyes now," the little girl's voice continued before she turned her eyes to watch the ground procedures out her window as the plane slowed and reversed its powerful engines. "My name's Diane," she offered. "What's yours?"

"Eva," the woman replied.

Eva let out a silent sigh and released her armrests, placing her trembling hands in her lap. She'd done it! She'd actually gotten on a plane and taken a flight of several hours—and survived. She chuckled softly in self-derision.

The little girl turned back to her, her own head tilted, and raised her brows. "What's so funny?" she asked.

"Oh...I was just thinking what a big baby I'm being about this trip. I should be more like you. You're not afraid to travel alone," Eva observed.

"I was the first time," the little girl said. "I thought my daddy wasn't going to be here to meet me."

Eva smiled at the self-assurance of the youngster, so adult in so small a person. And it was ironic that at ten years of age Diane Maxwell had so much confidence, while twenty-nine-year-old Eva Duncan could have used a little more.

Starting to relax again now that the plane was safely on the ground, Eva was once more amazed at the determination with which she'd set about taking this trip, her very first vacation, all by herself. She could still hear her mother lamenting her daughter's lack of good sense. Cautioning Eva that there were far too many plane crashes these days, Florence Stewart tried to persuade her youngest child and only daughter that a bus trip to Philadelphia would serve the same purpose. That it was unnecessary to fly all the way to God knows where just to have an adventure. But Eva had remained firm. She wanted this trip to someplace new, someplace far away. And no one knew better than she that lives could be lost on the ground far easier than in the air.

Eva straightened the elastic neck and long, full sleeves on her white peasant blouse and smoothed the front of her red slim skirt, hoping her outfit didn't look too wrinkled after three and a half hours in close quarters. She absently swept her hands over the short hair from front to back several times, fluffing it and feeling the curls spring into place with new life. Her toffee-colored face with its rounded soft cheeks and small rounded chin began to glow with the beginnings of excitement. Her brown eyes with their almond shape were bright and wide open, and her small mouth smiled gently. Eva looked over the head of her companion and also peered out onto the sunny afternoon as the plane taxied downfield and came to a stop.

Eva frowned, expecting to see a modern, sterile airport and terminal building, but could only see a rather old, dreary-looking hangar.

Diane settled back in her seat and sighed. She began to swing a leg back and forth over the edge of her seat in growing impatience to be off the plane.

"Do you always travel alone, Diane?" Eva asked.

Diane nodded, a pinky finger stuck into the side of her mouth and gnawed on absently by her small white teeth. "My mama doesn't like to fly. She's scared more than you are!" she enlightened Eva.

Still, Eva couldn't really imagine ever sending a child of her own on a trip like this alone.

"She says she can't leave my stepfather and stepbrother. Robert is still a baby," Diane announced.

At the beginning of the trip down to the U.S. Virgin Islands, Diane had been filled with impatience to see her father. Now that it was the end of school for the summer, she would be spending two weeks with him. It had been nearly a year since she'd last seen him, but she spoke of her father with gladness and love as though she saw him every day of her life. Eva wondered about a father that could inspire such devotion from so far away for fifty weeks of the year.

Diane informed Eva that her parents had divorced when she was a little girl. That had brought a smile to Eva's lips, because Diane was still so obviously a little girl. At ten she was still a bit chubby with baby fat. Her thick wavy hair was pulled back into a ponytail and gently twisted. Her brown face for the moment was round, but once the fat was lost and she grew some more, it would be more square with very attractive features.

Earlier when Eva asked Diane what her father did in the Virgin Islands, she'd responded that he studied fish. That had puzzled Eva, but she didn't have a chance to find out more as their lunch was served at that moment.

Over lunch, however, Diane regaled Eva with stories of the other times she'd visited her father, except for the one summer when he was away somewhere else, so her mother had sent her to summer camp. She hadn't enjoyed that nearly so much, but it was clear to Eva that at ten Diane Maxwell had experienced quite a lot.

Now as they gathered their carry-on luggage and prepared to leave the plane, Eva realized that she was about to leave a circumstance she'd gotten used to for almost four hours, to begin the next unfamiliar phase of her six-week vacation. The one hundred and thirty-eight passengers began filing out of the plane.

"Now we have to get our luggage," Diane said over

her shoulder informatively, looking up into Eva's face as they started down the stairway of the plane.

The heat was unexpected and fierce. It hit Eva full force as she crossed the runway to a sheltered walkway that took the passengers into the Harry S. Truman Airport and to their luggage. Diane walked with knowledge and ease toward the hangar, and Eva could only follow behind. She knew that after she got her luggage she was to take a cab to the boat docks at Red Hook on the other side of St. Thomas. From there she was to catch a ferry to St. John, the smallest of the three Virgin Islands and just twenty minutes away. That much seemed enough to worry about for the time being.

The dark, but cool, interior of the hangar was a sudden, welcome change to the heat. Eva hoped that she would adjust quickly. She thought ruefully that if she wanted unbearable summer heat and humidity, she could have stayed home in New Jersey.

She followed behind the other passengers to a motionless conveyor belt, and assumed that eventually her luggage would come this way. Diane, standing next to her, was craning her neck around the old, oddly converted hangar, obviously searching out her father.

"Are you sure he's going to meet you?" Eva asked the little girl in some concern.

"Yes..." Diane answered, giving up the search for the moment. "Sometimes he's late, but he always comes," she said positively. She looked up to Eva with a frown. "Isn't anybody going to meet you?"

"I'm afraid not. I...I don't know anybody here. This is my first time, remember?"

"But what hotel are you staying at?"

"I'm not staying at a hotel. I'm renting a house for my vacation."

"All by yourself?" Diane asked, eyes wide open.

"All by myself," Eva confirmed, nodding with a smile.

"I'd be scared. 'Specially at night," Diane confessed. The smile on Eva's face went through a transition totally lost on the little girl. It grew sad and rather pensive, her eyes distant and staring, its depths sudden dark pools hiding pain from the past.

"You get used to it," Eva murmured. She quickly pulled herself together and smiled down at Diane. "Maybe I'll see you around while you're here," Eva suggested.

Diane nodded in agreement. "You might get into trouble all by yourself. Maybe my father and I should keep an eye on you. Just in case."

Eva laughed lightly. "That's very nice of you, but I think I'll be okay."

Eva liked Diane's open friendliness, her thoughts of other people. She must have really wonderful parents, Eva imagined, even though their marriage hadn't worked and they separated. They were both doing something right with this youngster.

For a long time Eva used to compare every little girl she saw to Gail, her daughter. Every little body with two fat pigtails used to make her stop in midstride to stare and wonder, to feel her stomach tighten and eyes mist. It had taken a while to reconcile herself to the fact that there had been only one Gail, and she was gone.

Eva blinked and took a deep breath. She passed a slightly shaking hand over her damp forehead. It suddenly seemed so very warm in the hangar.

The conveyor belt churned into motion, and the passengers from her flight pushed to the edge in a rush, everyone anxious for his bags so each could continue on his way. Eva spotted her brown nylon duffle with its yellow luggage tag and reached to swing it off the conveyor to the floor. Her thirty-six-inch case came next, but she was not prepared for the weight and couldn't move it. She had to let go of the handle as the bag remained on the belt and went on a journey around the system again.

A tall blond youth, probably a college student, helped her the next time the bag came, and she thanked him. But she still had no idea how she'd manage everything by herself. As Eva stood in indecision, the blond young man again came to her rescue.

"You look like you could still use some help," he said good-naturedly. Eva smiled ruefully, looking down helplessly at her bags.

"I guess I do. I'm wondering how to get all of this to a taxi. For that matter, where do I find a taxi?"

"That's easy," the young man answered, the tropic breeze ruffling up his long shaggy hair. "The taxi depot is just through that door." He jerked a thumb over his shoulder. And then without any apparent effort he lifted the one oversized suitcase and her duffle. "If you have everything else, I'll walk you over."

"Oh, I really appreciate this!" Eva said with feeling, lifting her heavy tote onto her arm.

"No problem. You've never been here before?" he asked, adjusting his lanky, long-legged steps to her slower, shorter ones.

"No. This is my first time."

He chuckled. "Everybody packs too much the first time down here."

"But I'm going to be here for six weeks!" Eva said as they once more walked into the brilliant, startling sunshine. The youth shook his head as he put her bags down on the curb.

"You don't need much on the islands. You'll probably be in a bathing suit most of the time anyway. I bet you won't wear half the stuff you brought with you."

Feeling already as though she was way overdressed in her blouse and skirt and open-toed sandals and with perspiration making trails down the valley of her breasts and down her back, she could well believe him.

"At any rate, I want to thank you for your help. It was kind of you."

"Sure…anytime." He smiled, standing with his hands on his narrow hips.

"Are you on vacation?" Eva asked.

"Sort of. I work here," he answered.

"What kind of work?"

He laughed. "The easy kind, and as little as possible! I come down every summer and work at the resort on St. John. I teach the guests how to snorkel, use the Sunfish, and how to surf sail…"

Eva raised her brow. She didn't know what he was talking about. She smiled, however, at his enthusiasm and obvious enjoyment of what he did.

"It doesn't pay very much," he continued. "But it's worth it just to be here for the three months!" He started backing toward the door and away from her. "If you ever get over to Caneel, ask for Tim. I'll take you out for a sail or something!"

Eva laughed, her almond eyes closing to slits filled with surprising merriment. "I'll remember. Thanks again for your help. And have a good summer!"

"Yeah…you, too!" He waved once, turning back into the hangar.

The sound of male laughter brought Eva's head around, and she squinted against the sun into a group of three black men obviously discussing her. Wondering if she was already headed for trouble, she watched uncomfortably as one of the men of medium height with a dark angular face beaming with a smile walked over to her. His white teeth flashed in his face, even and bright, his mustache under a broadly flared nose almost the color of his ebony skin.

"You want taxi, lady?" he asked softly in a lilting voice, the accent new to Eva's ears. But he had said the right words.

"Yes, I do." Eva smiled back. The other two men, watching the encounter, began to talk excitedly to themselves, laughing softly. Eva wished she knew what the joke was.

"Where you go, eh?" the man asked her now. Eva came to attention and dug in her purse for her crumpled sheet of instructions.

"Oh...ah...I have to get to Red Hook...to the ferry." She looked at him uncertainly, hoping he knew where she meant. She was relieved when he only nodded and reached for the bags at her feet. He swung them into the back seat of a spacious cab and then helped Eva in, closing the door. It was only then that Eva remembered Diane Maxwell and let out a small exclamation as she looked out the window toward the passengers exiting the building used as a terminal. She'd gotten so involved in her own arrangements that she'd forgotten all about the little girl. As the cab pulled away from the curb, Eva hoped that Diane's father had arrived and that the little girl was safe. For that matter, as her driver saluted the friends he was leaving behind and they cackled at him in passing, Eva hoped that she herself was safe.

It was almost a full ten minutes into the ride before Eva allowed herself to sit back in the cab seat and let the warm breeze blowing through the open windows of the car cool her. She had trouble with the fact that the cars on St. Thomas drove on the left-hand side of the road. Eva kept expecting that at any moment they'd crash head on into an oncoming vehicle.

"You here for a vacation?" her still-grinning driver asked.

"Yes." Eva answered shortly, not volunteering anything more, much more used to the morose type of cab-drivers of New York than to this extrovert driving her across the island.

"Where you stay? Red Hook is only a ferry dock, you know."

"I know. I have to take a ferry from there to St. John."

He sucked through his teeth and shook his head frowning at her in his rearview mirror. "What you go to St. John for? It too quiet over there. No nightlife. No music."

"That's just fine," Eva nodded. "I don't want nightlife. I want peace and quiet."

"Naw…you too pretty for peace and quiet," the driver declared. "You want to have a good time, yes?"

"Of course…"

"Then you listen to Deacon, yes? You stay on St. Thomas. Everything happenin' right here! Lots of restaurants. You like to shop? All women like to spend money. Best shops right here."

Eva laughed at his cheerful persistence, but didn't argue with him. The car was passing down a stretch of street that left a dock on her right with a small island about a half mile in the distance. To her left in the distance were the mountains of St. Thomas, spotted with houses built into its side, whitewashed with pink and red roofs. Along the roadway where they now moved were a few hotels and lots of shops and restaurants just as

Deacon had mentioned. The tourists, predominantly young couples dressed in shorts and T-shirts with cameras hanging from their shoulders and very red skins obviously overexposed to the tropic sun too quickly, sauntered along the street window-shopping.

"That's Charlotte Amalie," her driver supplied. "It's our capital and main center. The cruise ships come in every week and it gets very crowded with people."

But within minutes they were past the main street with its nineteenth-century fortlike structures and heading up the winding roads into the hills. Eva was enjoying this first swift look at the island.

"You by yourself?" the driver inquired, interrupting her peaceful thoughts.

"Yes, I am," Eva answered.

"No good! You need someone show you around the island," he said in his odd musical voice. All the words seemed rounder than what Eva was used to, but she could understand him.

"I'm sure I'll be okay," she demured, already guessing what he was leading up to.

He grinned. "Pretty lady like you have to be careful."

"I won't get into any trouble," Eva assured him. "I came to rest, sit on the beach and read a lot…"

"Agh! Why you want to do that for?" he exclaimed in disgust. "You listen to me, lady. I can show you good time."

"I bet you could," Eva said caustically with a touch of amused insight into the man. Nevertheless he laughed heartily at her skepticism. Eva took that moment to change the subject.

"What time does the ferry leave from Red Hook?"

"On the hour. Next ferry"—he looked down at his watch quickly—"at four o'clock. Maybe we make it."

He shrugged with a total lack of concern with whether or not they would. But Eva didn't relish the idea of sitting around for an hour waiting for the five o'clock boat. She was tired and felt like she'd been traveling the entire day and still hadn't reached her final destination. She was sticky and very much wanted a shower and time to relax.

"Where you stay on St. John? Caneel?" Deacon asked. Eva didn't expect to see the man again, so she told him.

"No...I'm renting a house on the island. I believe it overlooks Hawksnest Bay."

"Yes. Very pretty there. But you get lonely. You see. You come back to St. Thomas and visit Deacon. I show you all around my island. You have good time!"

Eva merely smiled at the offer, her innate feminine suspicions aroused.

"Maybe I marry you, yes?" Deacon declared. Then he again burst into laughter at the shocked, wide-eyed expression on Eva's face. Subtlety is totally unknown to this man, Eva thought in wry amusement, turning her head to look out the window and hoping to discourage further conversation as to her vacation plans.

The landscape and setting seemed to be at odd variance with the development apparently taking place all over the island. For every lopsided or run-down house there was a rich, modern condominium or resort hotel. The hotels seemed almost out of place in the lush rolling hills that opened up frequently to give a spectacular view of the sea. But the tourist trade was the major business in these string of small islands dotting the Caribbean Sea. Eva had been told that the water was the most fantastic blue she'd ever see, and it was true. It looked as if tons of powdered turquoise had been dumped into the water to give it a pale translucent aqua color that was almost unreal. For the rest of the twenty-minute ride, Eva was absorbed by the beauty of it all.

Suddenly the car came to a stop inside a fenced dock and Deacon climbed out to help her with her luggage. There was a blue-and-white boat against the dock, filled with people and baggage and boxes.

"Is that the ferry?" Eva asked anxiously as a bell rang twice from the upper deck of the craft, announcing its imminent departure.

"That's it," Deacon said, still not hurrying. But some silent communication was apparently transmitted as the boat made no move to pull away, and Deacon approached it with Eva's luggage as Eva ran to catch up to him, struggling with the heavy carry-on tote, her purse, and a camera.

Two teenage boys silently took the bags from Deacon and swung them without care onto an already heaped pile of baggage in the center of the deck. Eva dug to pull money from her purse to pay the cabdriver.

"Thank you..." she breathed, shrugging her camera strap back up her arm and picking up the tote.

"You come see Deacon on St. Thomas...anytime," he said and grinned, touching his forehead in a respectful gesture to her.

Eva turned back to the boat, which had already started its engines. A space was beginning to yawn between the dock edge and the side of the boat. She stood looking apprehensive as the ferry gave every sign of leaving with her luggage while she stood foolishly on the dock afraid to jump the widening space.

No one appeared to have noticed her predicament until a quiet, incredibly deep voice said from the boat, "Step over this way...here."

Then Eva was aware of a hand and arm reaching out

to her, but her eyes remained focused on the space below her revealing the deep blue water of the bay. Suddenly, something hooked her violently around the waist, and she was hauled unceremoniously from the dock edge to the deck of the boat. She drew in a sharp breath of surprise, which was immediately forced out again when her body made jarring contact with the hard chest and thigh of a man who held her against him, her feet cleared of the wooden floorboards.

"Oh!" Eva let out, as she managed one hand up to his shoulder to steady herself. Her chest was flattened against his as he held her for a moment longer and peered silently into her stunned, upturned face. Slowly he set her down on her feet, her legs unsteady. When Eva continued to sway with the unfamiliar movement of the boat, the man maintained a firm hold around her waist. The contact made Eva feel weak-kneed for a second, but then he slid his hand away.

For no particular reason Eva was aware of the warm, musky smell of male perspiration of the man in the tropical heat. He was a big man and showed not the smallest sign of strain at having lifted her with her arms full from one level area to another.

His rugged square face with its prominent jaw and chin was closed and hard, and he didn't acknowledge Eva's breathy muttered thanks. She didn't realize she was staring, awestruck by a face that was not exactly handsome, but certainly strong and masculine. His brown skin was a bit darker than her own, and she was curiously drawn to the fact that his eyes seemed to be the same shade of brown, giving him a unique, intense staring look.

Eva felt a tug on her arm. Suddenly embarrassed, she looked round into the calm unsurprised eyes of Diane Maxwell.

"Diane! Hello again. I didn't know what had happened to you."

"My daddy was there to meet me," Diane offered logically, unconcerned that they'd parted company abruptly at the airport.

"Oh, I'm glad. Where is your father?" Eva asked, briefly looking around the other passengers.

"Here he is," Diane said, pointing to the tall man silently watching the exchange and Eva's rescuer of a moment before.

"Oh!" Eva breathed, swinging her eyes back and up to look once more into that imposing face. She collected herself and held out a hand.

"Hello, Mr. Maxwell. I'm Eva Duncan. Thank you for your assistance. I—I'm sorry I was so clumsy and slow…"

"Don't worry about it," he murmured a bit coldly, reluctantly taking Eva's proffered hand. Her smaller one was swallowed and firmly held briefly before he turned and lowered himself to a bench. He sat back to rest both arms outward along the back of the seat, one ankle resting on top of the other knee. He wore brown slacks, thong sandals, and a pale yellow shirt open halfway down the front.

Eva's eyes lowered hypnotically to the opening because of the dark curly mass of hair that was displayed. She'd never seen such a hairy chest. She frowned deeply at the thought and turned quickly back to Diane. The youngster was now kneeling on the bench facing her father and leaning over the side of the boat, letting the salty breeze blow into her face as the ferryboat gained full speed. Awkwardly Eva took the seat next to the little girl, putting her almost directly opposite Diane's father. Eva smiled briefly at him as she sat, but he didn't return the smile and, as a matter of fact, turned his head to look at the same view his daughter was enjoying, ignoring her.

He wasn't at all what Eva had expected Diane's father to be like, but then she hadn't given an awful lot of thought to it before. She hadn't thought he'd be so—so physical. His presence was almost overwhelming. Eva stole another surreptitious look at him, at the sculptured line of his profile with its wide full mouth and the strong long nose, at the neatly clipped and combed hair, at the incredible hair on his chest. She could only think in that instant that Kevin, her husband, had been so much smaller a man with very little body hair.

The eyes of the man sitting opposite her looked back to her, and again Eva resorted to a gentle smile.

"Your daughter is a much better traveler than I am," she confessed ruefully.

He stared at her long and hard, almost rudely, until Eva began to wonder if there was something wrong with the man. But again, his eyes shifted to look out over the sea, over his daughter's head with its wisps of hair being tugged upward in the wind. "She's had a lot of practice," he finally chose to answer and said no more.

Well! He certainly is not like his daughter, Eva thought as she gave up the idea of further conversation. Whatever it was Diane held so dear about her father was only known to Diane. Eva shrugged the thought away. It didn't matter, since she probably wouldn't be seeing them again during Diane's brief two-week stay anyway.

Eva took a moment to look around the small craft, noticing the mixture of people. There were those who were obviously just arriving for the start of vacation, with their pale untouched skins, and those who lived on these islands with their beige, brown, and black skin tones.

There was cargo of produce and dairy goods for delivery and boxes of what seemed to be tools and machine parts.

Diane, now bored with the scene from the boat, twisted to sit down next to Eva and let a big yawn stretch and distort her round face. Eva smiled at her and, totally unaware of the movement, moved her hand to smooth back the child's windblown hair.

"Are you tired?" she asked softly.

"A little," Diane admitted. "I'm hungry, too."

"Well…your father will probably give you dinner as soon as you get home."

"Do you want to have dinner with us?" Diane asked in a tired voice.

Eva didn't look again at the man opposite her, but his presence prompted her quick reply. "I don't think so, dear. You and your father will want to get to know each other again after a long year apart. And I'd like to get settled myself."

"Maybe another time, then," Diane said.

"Maybe," Eva responded, although doubting it. She looked up to find Diane's father staring openly at her. He didn't look away this time, but Eva did, disconcerted by his pale brown eyes. His gaze was frankly curious and intent on examining her. Unused to such open perusal of her person, Eva fidgeted on her seat. If he was aware of her discomfort, he made no sign as his gaze swept slowly over her body. Eva nervously brushed a hand over her short hair and fumbled with the loose neck of her blouse. She now wished she hadn't allowed herself to be talked into wearing so young and revealing an outfit. She didn't view herself as a slender young girl anymore, but a mature woman who should dress her own age.

The engines suddenly were cut, and the craft slowed until it was merely drifting into the dock at Cruz Bay on the island of St. John. Already the other passengers were standing and preparing to leave, gathering suitcases, bags, and boxes. A young girl, her hair cornrowed attractively over her head, collected the two-dollar fare from each departing person.

Revived once more and on the last leg of her trip, Diane jumped up and stood waiting for her father to dig out her two bags from the diminishing pile on deck. He tossed them onto the dock and returned to grab Eva's two bags. Then he turned to her.

"Thank you," Eva shouted, as she gingerly stepped from the boat to the dock, this time without assistance. Out of curiosity, Diane had moved to the back of the vessel, watching as the anchor was lowered and the ropes were secured on the dock. She leaned over to peer into the aqua water to see how far down the anchor would fall. She was leaning precariously forward when Eva saw her and let out a gasp. Diane's father never moved as his eyes turned to his daughter. He simply called sharply to her.

"Diane! Get away from there," he said brusquely in his deep voice and the little girl quickly obeyed. She came back to her father's side. He gave her a relatively small case.

"You know what the Jeep looks like. Why don't you go put that in?"

"Okay," she agreed readily and went off down the walkway, struggling with the case. "Bye, Eva!" she shouted once over her shoulder.

"She's a lovely little girl," Eva commented, but Diane's father didn't respond. Instead he turned to look rather forbiddingly down at her, his light brown eyes sweeping over her again, coming back to study her face.

"Is someone meeting you?"

Eva let out a low, nervous chuckle. "Someone is supposed to meet me, the agent for the house I'm leasing. Mildred Decker." He nodded once.

"She'll be here," he said confidently.

"Do you know her?" Eva asked.

"This is a very small island. You quickly get to know most people here." He picked up Diane's other bags and started to turn away. "She should be along any moment. Do you need any more help?" he asked a little archly, in a way that Eva took offense to.

"I'll be fine. Thank you for your assistance," she said formally, too tired to try and be friendly with the stiff, somewhat arrogant man.

He never said another word. Just nodded briefly and walked to meet his waiting daughter, who was standing by a red, canopied Jeep. Soon they were shooting off down the street away from the dock and out of Eva's sight. She wondered, nonetheless, where he lived.

"Are you Eva Duncan?"

Eva turned sideways to see a slight, graying woman of about fifty smiling at her. What a change from the last twenty minutes of Diane's father. The woman held out a fine-boned, wrinkled hand. "Hi. I'm Milly Decker. I see you made it with no mishaps. That's unusual the first time here," she laughed.

"I guess I was just lucky. I did have a lot of help since leaving the airport," Eva confessed, shaking hands with the very tanned woman with pale gray eyes in her lined face. Eva quickly went on to describe her encounter with the cabdriver, Deacon, causing Milly Decker to laugh.

"Oh, our cabdrivers are legendary. They are mostly very nice, and they have a keen eye for an attractive single lady."

Eva shook her head demurely. "It's nice of you to say

so." Between Milly and herself they got the bags to another Jeep, this one blue, waiting at the end of the dock.

"This is the town of Cruz Bay," Milly explained as they headed slowly out of town. She pointed out various shops, businesses, and points of interest. Then they were quickly climbing into the hills, curving away from the town receding below them.

"Martin Isaacs called me long distance to let me know you were coming."

"It was very generous of Mr. Isaacs and his wife to let me use their house for six weeks."

"They are really lovely people. But that house means a lot to them. They only let very special people come here."

Eva smiled. "I'm not that special, but I do enjoy working for Mr. Isaacs. Since he and his wife were going to be in Europe the whole summer, it was he who suggested I use my vacation this way."

"Some vacation," Milly Decker said in an envious voice. "I wish I could take six weeks!"

"Well, I actually only get three weeks. I'm taking the additional three without pay."

"Well, I hope that he gave you a good deal on the cost of the lease."

"Oh, he did. I'm paying less here than I do for rent at home. This trip is costing me very little."

"That's fantastic. I do hope you enjoy it here, and I hope you won't be too lonely on that hillside. There's another house about a half mile down the road from you, but closer to the beach. It's occupied by a marine biologist, Adam Maxwell. You can always call on him if you have any problems. He knows the island, and he's good in an emergency."

"Maxwell…" Eva mouthed, wondering. "I met a Mr. Maxwell on the ferry ride over here."

Milly Decker laughed. "See what I mean? Sounds like Maxwell. I believe he went into St. Thomas to pick up his daughter, or something like that."

"Yes, that's right. His daughter Diane is spending vacation with him."

Eva was finding she had to hold firmly to the side of her seat or risk falling out on the incredible winding road. The island of St. John was much more scenic, lush, and green than St. Thomas. Despite the cabdriver's claim to the contrary, St. John gave the appearance of being more the kind of place she had in mind in which to rest and relax for several weeks.

Two years ago when she went to work for the law firm of Berger Isaacs, Eva wanted to lose herself in the complicated work of the office. She didn't want any time to think about her past, to grieve and lament and wish it all undone. It was important that she continue with her life and make it the very best she could for herself alone. But she had used her job as legal secretary and law clerk to bury herself, to stop feeling, to think of nothing but her work. It was her boss, Martin Isaacs, who'd convinced her she was too valuable to the firm and to herself to run herself into the ground with overwork. So, for the first time in her life, she was on a real vacation.

Every time the car came around another bend, another semicircular aqua bay was exposed to Eva's view. She didn't realize that any place in the world could really be so lovely, and she was suddenly very glad she was here. She was looking forward to the next six weeks.

"Do you drive?" Milly asked her now.

"Yes, I do. I've never driven a Jeep before, but…"

"There's nothing to it. You'll probably have more

trouble adjusting to driving on the left-hand side and on the steep hills and sharp turns. But you can't get anywhere on the island without your own transportation. I've arranged for you to pick one up tomorrow.''

"Thank you. That would be helpful.''

"Also I've already put food in the house, so you won't have to starve tonight.''

"Oh, you didn't have to go to so much trouble!''

Milly Decker smiled good-naturedly. "Well, as I said, Martin Isaacs says to take good care of you. And there are lots of people to get in touch with if you get too lonely. There are several good restaurants on the island if you get tired of your own cooking. One place shows movies every Saturday night. Sometimes the National Park Service here sponsors talks and tours. The nights can sometimes be the worst. There's a radio, of course, and newspapers, but not much TV if you're used to that. If you get too lonely, give Maxwell a call.''

Eva seriously doubted if she'd get so lonely as to do that, but she remained silent on the subject.

"Also, Troy Hamilton and his family live in the other direction from Maxwell's place. Troy does odd jobs for the resorts here, and his wife Trina runs one of the food stands in town. There's a mess of kids in that family, ages eight to twenty-eight. But they're nice people.''

The car swung off the smooth paved road and onto a more rocky one, stopping a hundred feet later at the base of cement steps. The steps appeared to lead up to the side of a house set back into the hillside. The sun was beginning its descent, and the sky was a glorious shade of orange in the west. Now that she'd finally arrived, Eva allowed the exhaustion she felt to begin to steal over her. She hoped the bed was firm and comfortable.

Milly Decker showed her around the three-and-a-half-room structure. It contained a long spacious gallery opened on one side to face Hawksnest Bay and the west. At one end of the gallery was a small screened-in kitchen. Through another screened door and window in the wall of the gallery was a large sitting room and bedroom, and somewhere at the end of the bedroom was a bath. It was a clever and efficiently built structure allowing for air to circulate freely throughout and lots of late afternoon sunshine, as well as offering protection from the nighttime rain and storms.

Milly Decker, seeing her young client's fatigue, cut short her visit, promising to come by for Eva the next morning and take her to pick up her rented Jeep. Then she departed.

In the late afternoon silence surrounding her, Eva stood on the strange deck with its missing one side and looked out over this impossible land of make-believe. She wondered if Kevin would have liked this. She wondered if Gail would have liked Diane. They would have been just about the same age. But then she reasoned that if things were different, she wouldn't be here at all.

Leaving her bags where they were, Eva elected to shower, put on a short cotton nightgown, and crawl into bed with a glass of orange juice from the well-stocked kitchen. But the juice went untouched as she lay on the cool sheets of the queen-size bed, exhaustion and sleep fast overtaking her. She could hear the evening breeze rustling playfully through the tree leaves and the gentle lap of water swishing over the edge of a sandy beach.

Eva wondered if she could walk to the beach from the cottage. Did she remember to bring a beach hat and moisturizing lotion? She wondered if Adam Maxwell ever smiled and what he would look like if he did.

And then she was asleep.

Chapter Two

From under the protective shield of a seagrape tree, Eva had a good view of the rest of the world. She could watch the sun crystalize and crack the surface of the water so that it shimmered and sparkled like gems. She could see the two- and single-masted schooners, the cutters, and the catboats sailing in and out of the bay, and the small motor launches skimming with great speed between two points. Sometimes, if she was very still and alert, a fish would jump, arch its body for a split second, then disappear beneath the water's surface. There was even a resident pelican who would periodically take off with a great flapping of its wings to circle once around the bay and then nose-dive with incredible force into the water after his meal of small fish.

Eva was just amazed. This place was so far removed from New Jersey and what she'd been used to all her life that even after three days, she couldn't believe it was real. It was hard to think that people lived year round in this almost-perfect spot. How did they manage to get anything done? There wasn't anything she had definitely planned to accomplish while here. There were ten paperback novels to read and some crocheting she could do.

Maybe she'd use her camera. But there didn't seem to be any rush. Six weeks was a long time.

She wiggled back comfortably into her portable seat, a mere construction of chrome bars and canvas that gave firm support to her bottom and back. She stretched out her shapely brown legs and dug her toes luxuriously into the warm silky sand. She loosened the ribbon tie on her short white terry cover-up, showing a little of the tangerine one-piece tank suit beneath. It was the most comfortable and convenient thing to wear, but she'd yet to venture into the water with it on. It was just so much easier to sit like this, with her short-brimmed straw hat, cute but not lending much protection to her face, perched on her head and her tortoiseshell sunglasses protecting her eyes.

The first time she'd found her way to the beach, the day after her arrival, there'd been a small sailing craft at one of the moorings in the bay. A small launch from shore had gone out to it and back to shore again, and after a while Eva could distinguish the figures of Diane Maxwell and her father. She'd been tempted to go over and say hello, but two things stopped her. One was the feeling that Adam Maxwell wasn't particularly friendly, and the other was that Diane should have the time alone with her father. So Eva had sat in curiosity, watching them from afar. While Diane splashed and swam with obvious ability, her father seemed to be making repairs to the craft, loading small tanks and trunks, swim fins, and other equipment Eva couldn't identify. Then he'd call to Diane, who'd climb into the launch, and they'd motor to the larger sailing ship. The ship would then pull out of the bay, and they were gone the rest of the afternoon.

The next day the procedure was the same, except that

when they returned later in the afternoon, there was a third person with them…a woman, but Eva couldn't tell how young or old she was. She could not curb, however, the curiosity that questioned the presence of this other person, even while she knew it was none of her concern.

Now as she sat with the unread book on her lap, she realized that she hadn't seen Diane or her father yet, but the sailing vessel with its distinct pale blue hull was in its usual place.

It was nearly one o'clock in the afternoon when Eva saw the familiar two figures appear with the woman of the previous day. Eva watched as a box and gear were loaded into the launch; then the woman stood to the side as an observer while Adam Maxwell held a discussion with his daughter. Eva could tell from Diane's defiant gestures that it was an argument more than a discussion, and Diane was very likely losing. Suddenly she turned and started marching angrily down the beach toward the end where Eva sat. Eva watched as Adam Maxwell stood with legs braced apart, fists on his hips, and yelled after the small angry figure.

"Diane! Come back here!"

Diane continued, coming so close to where Eva sat that Eva could see the tears on the little girl's face. She had on a red-white-and-blue-striped swimsuit and a T-shirt over it. Her hair was parted evenly, and twisted into knots over either ear.

Eva's eyes moved from Diane back down the beach to her father and back to Diane again. She put her sunglasses and hat down and stood up, brushing sand from her legs.

"Diane…" she called out softly. She had to call a second time before the youngster stopped in puzzlement and looked in her direction. Adam Maxwell was already

tured in the vague direction of one end of the open bay. "I have some algae and sea grass to collect. It should take about an hour…"

Eva smiled at him reassuringly. "We'll be fine. I'll just sit on the sand and read for a while. Diane can swim or explore."

"You can go swimming, too."

"I'm afraid I don't swim very well." Eva grinned ruefully, remembering her brother's futile attempts to teach her, even though she wasn't afraid of the water. Maxwell studied her speculatively for a moment, murmured, "Ummmmm," and scratched his fingertips idly through the covering of hair on his chest. Eva's eyes were drawn to the motion.

"In any case, the water isn't very deep here. I don't think you'll get into trouble," he said sarcastically. Eva stiffened, wondering if he was being patronizing. There was a noisy splash behind them. They turned to see that Diane had already begun to entertain herself.

"Diane is a good swimmer. Just don't let her go out too far."

"Of course not," Eva agreed, irritated with him again. He turned away. "I'll see you in a while."

"Be careful," Eva said after him, without thinking, and before she could stop herself. It had been as natural as saying hello or good-bye. Adam stopped in his movements of getting into the launch again to look at her. Eva turned from his quizzical stare, lifted the tote, and moved it farther into the cool shelter of the shrubbery. Behind her she could hear the starting of the launch motor and the boat proceeding slowly to the spot Maxwell had pointed out. Sitting in the shade, Eva squinted with curiosity into the distance to watch as Diane's father dipped a pail repeatedly into the water, hoisted it aboard to make selections, and emptied the rest back into the sea. At one point he put on a face mask and fins and went over the side to dive deep beneath the surface. He stayed down longer than Eva imagined it was possible to do. She was not at all conscious of the breath she held or the clenching of her fists as she waited for him to surface. When he did, she relaxed and turned her attention to Diane.

Diane looked as though she was having a great deal of fun, and Eva wished that she could enjoy the cool clear water as well. She walked into the edge of the water up to her knees, while Diane dove, swam, somersaulted, and generally showed off for her amused audience. Eva soon suggested lunch and together they sat drinking bottled orange juice and eating salad.

It was almost two hours before Maxwell returned. He declined lunch but quickly went through two bottles of the juice. Then he began to sort and divide his samples. Diane knelt next to him in obvious curiosity. As she put away the extra salad, Eva watched father and daughter as they sat so close to each other in the sand. Diane had her father's coloring and, for that matter, much of his facial structure. Eva could begin to see the resemblance in the mouth particularly, the nose, and the jaw. Diane was going to be very pretty in five or six years' time. Eva wondered how much the little girl also resembled her mother.

"How many times do I have to tell you not to touch that?" Adam's voice broke into Eva's speculations. Her eyes cleared, and she focused on an annoyed Adam and a pouting, frustrated Diane.

Eva moved closer to them in the sand. Maxwell looked up at her. Eva smiled at Diane and looked back to Adam. "I'm like Diane. I'm very curious, too." She paused to let her comment take hold.

"What is all this stuff?" She waved a hand over Adam's open sea chest and its mixture of seaweeds and shells. "Maybe you can explain so Diane and I can understand?"

She was not prepared for his jaw suddenly tensing in what looked to be anger. Eva could only guess that he didn't appreciate her interference or the interruptions. He turned, however, back to Diane and frowned.

"Do you really want to know about all this?" he asked skeptically.

"Oh, yes!" Diane breathed.

Maxwell looked at Eva and quirked a brow. But then he did start to explain what he had taken from the blue waters of the bay. Eva sat back, watching. When it was apparent that Diane was not at all bored by her father's talk of turtle grass, sandy bottoms, and plankton, Maxwell identified all the things she was pointing to. Adam warmed to his subject and didn't notice for a full fifteen minutes that only Diane was asking questions. He looked up finally at Eva, but she was sitting with her legs gracefully tucked under her, watching the growing animation on Diane's face.

"Daddy, what's this?" Diane asked, fearlessly lifting a piece of delicate-looking growth that resembled a leaf but was stiffer, harder, and lilac in color.

"That's a fan coral."

"It's really pretty," Diane exclaimed.

"This is just a small piece that was broken off. The larger ones are even nicer."

"How come you didn't get a bigger piece then?"

"Because I don't want to break off a healthy piece of coral. All the reef waters around these islands are protected by law. You're not supposed to take sea life out of it."

Diane frowned. "But you do."

Adam pursed his lips at her logic. "Well…yeah, you're right. But I study it all so I can help keep it the way it is. Or make it better. I don't take just for the sake of taking. That would be wrong."

Diane thought about that. "My teacher said that studying the sea is important."

"She's right," Adam agreed, impressed that Diane remembered.

"She says that people po…pol…"

"Pollute," Adam supplied.

"Yeah…polluting the water and killing all the fish and plants. Is that true?"

"I'm afraid so, Diane. But we're also studying the sea for new sources of food and energy…"

Diane wrinkled her nose. "I don't really like fish very much to eat, but I think it would be fun to study them," she decided.

Adam looked hard at his daughter. Diane, unaware of his contemplation, carefully lifted a starfish from a shallow dish of water. The deeply textured golden brown surface of the sea creature was hard and stiff to the touch.

"What are you going to do with this?" Diane asked.

"Well…starfish are pretty, but they're also a nuisance. They compete with other fish for food at the bottom of the sea. I want to see how a starfish can be used either for food or maybe in some other way."

Diane examined the underside, Adam showing a growing admiration at his daughter's lack of squeamishness at handling the unfamiliar creature and her interest.

"Be careful! If we don't hurt it, I can return it to the sea later." Diane slowly replaced the starfish in its dish. Growing curious herself, Eva pointed to a green shiny plant and asked Adam what he hoped to learn from it.

He began to explain the research being done on the sea-weed. This man loves his work, Eva realized. She was captivated by the gentle, caring way in which he handled the collected sea life in front of him. She wondered if he was ever so kind to people. Maxwell suddenly sat back on his heels.

"Anyway…enough biology for the day." Some of his animation disappeared, but at least, Eva thought, she'd found there was more to him than just the hard, cold outer shell.

"Daddy…" Diane began hesitantly. Maxwell turned his light brown eyes to gaze at Diane.

"Well?" he prompted.

"Remember you said that sometime you'd show me how to snorkel? Could we do it now?" she asked.

Eva could see the refusal forming on his mouth, his head beginning to shake negatively.

"That does sound like fun," Eva contributed. Maxwell turned rather stony eyes to her. Eva merely smiled mischievously. "Then you can help your father in his research. Be an assistant."

"Could I?" Diane asked, wide-eyed. Maxwell was beginning to look uncomfortable and also as though he was regretting having Eva along.

Well, that's just too bad, Eva decided. He has a lifetime with his daughter, and he'd better learn to understand her. Eva grinned in amusement at his indecision.

Adam looked at his daughter's breathless, eager expression and stood up in the sand, towering over them both. "Okay…" he agreed slowly and turned a hard triumphant look to Eva. "And you're coming, too," he added.

Eva's eyes flew open and her mouth dropped in

stunned surprise while Diane was busy hopping all over the place in joy.

"But..." Eva began.

"I'll get the masks and fins," Maxwell said, enjoying having turned the tables on her. He dug around in the launch and came up with an armful of ominous-looking black rubber objects.

Diane stood eagerly, waiting for Maxwell to give her equipment and looking up at her father with so much love that Eva's heart jumped in her chest at the adoration. But her feelings of support for Diane did nothing to release the nervous tension inside her. She chewed on her bottom lip.

"Maxwell..." she began in what she hoped was a calm, persuasive voice. "I don't swim. Remember?"

He frowned impatiently at her, his square jaw jutting stubbornly. "Can you float with your face in the water?"

Eva nodded suspiciously.

"Good! That's all you need to know," he said in a deep, amused voice and thrust three strange-looking objects at her. Eva grabbed them and opened her mouth to say something more in protest, but Maxwell ignored her, picking up his own things and heading for the edge of the water.

"Come on, Eva!" Diane commanded anxiously, half afraid that her father would still change his mind.

Feeling her stomach knot, Eva walked slowly behind Diane into the water and again up to her knees. Maxwell attached his hose to the side of his face mask. Using his own saliva to clean the clear glass of the mask, he then quickly rinsed it in the salty aqua water. He then placed the tight elastic band around his head, making a wide indentation in his soft tightly curled hair, the mask resting for the moment on his forehead. Diane watched, imitating him, and Maxwell murmured to her as he helped adjust the tightness of the band. He turned to Eva and stopped cold. He raised a sardonic brow, and a chuckle rumbled deep in his chest.

"Don't you think you'd better take that off first?" he asked, pointing to her. Eva looked down at her cover-up. She inadvertently grabbed the neckline closed.

Adam saw her hesitation, perhaps even recognized it for what it was. But he was firm and unsympathetic. "You have to take it off."

Eva put her gear down and with stiff fingers untied the ribbon closures. She turned her back to Maxwell as she slipped the cover-up off her shoulders and tossed it onto the sand. A wave of warm blood infused her cheeks, and she felt suddenly as though she had the most unattractive body in the world with all her worst points outlined. Only after she'd retrieved her things did Eva dare to raise her eyes to Maxwell's steady gaze. She couldn't begin to interpret what she saw. Curiosity. Surprise. A kind of sparkle in his eyes. Admiration? She only knew his jaw suddenly twitched and his eyes seemed dark and veiled. He stood looking at her so seductively, so long, that Eva came very close to giving him back his things, rescuing her cover-up, and, despite Diane, absolutely refusing to go.

But in a low voice he began explaining to both her and Diane how to wear the mask and the fins. He explained that all they had to do was keep the open end of the air hose above the water and breathe fairly slowly through the mouthpiece. Then he showed them what to do if water got into the air hose or if it filled the mask.

"Now...I'll stay between you and hold on to you. If you have any trouble, squeeze my hand. Okay? I won't go into water so deep that you won't be able to stand up. Are you ready?''

"I'm ready," Diane said, already moving into the water until it was up to her neck.

So far as Eva was concerned, Adam still had not said anything to make her feel any better. But he took her hand firmly in his own and began to move into the water. Eva gripped as if her life depended on it. She followed suit as Maxwell and Diane put their mouthpieces in. Diane took her father's outstretched hand, and slowly Maxwell fell forward into a prone position, bringing his daughter and Eva down with him.

Eva clutched convulsively on Maxwell's hand. Suddenly her face was in the water and she could see the sandy bottom of the sea. Her feet floated up behind her, and she seemed held up and buoyed by the water. She was breathing heavily and feeling odd, light-headed. It seemed as if so much air was filling her lungs and taking so long to go out. She realized she was breathing too deeply and unnaturally. She forced herself to slow down.

She had given no thought to her hair and could feel the water all around, making the straight short strands feather out into the sea. And all other considerations were ignored as Eva allowed her initial panic to subside, and she realized she was actually looking under the sea at the wonderful world it presented. It was so clear that it was like not being underwater at all, except for the strange and colorful array of fish and plants, the rock and coral formation. Automatically Eva began to gently kick her feet and found that the slow movements would propel her forward in the water.

She couldn't believe that she, Eva Duncan, was actually doing this. It seemed unreal, a fantasy. She, who couldn't swim, was watching the underwater of the Caribbean Sea move magically past her.

Maxwell occasionally turned his head in her direction but continued to hold her hand and to take the lead in directing them. He moved toward a low crop of dead coral covered with black, round, spindle-type objects. Eva saw one particularly large fish, which made her nervous, circling around them for a while. But Maxwell showed no signs of concern, so she tried not to either.

Eva lost track of time and reality, lost all sense of the past. This was new, and it made her new. She had dared to venture forth into the unknown and she loved it. She was suddenly very grateful that Maxwell hadn't given her an out from this experience. It was beyond description.

It seemed as if they had only just started, when Eva realized that Maxwell was slowly heading back into shore. He stood up and pulled them both to their feet.

"I don't believe this!" Eva exclaimed, breathless. "That was…really something!" She brushed the wet hair from her forehead. "I've never seen such pretty fish. Maxwell, there was one big one…"

"Barracuda," he responded, pushing his mask to his forehead.

"Bar—barracuda," Eva said weakly. In her mind and limited knowledge of such things, barracudas were grouped with man-eating sharks.

"For the most part, they just leave you alone," Maxwell explained. "But they don't like anyone or anything messing around their territory. He was just following to make sure we were just…passing through."

Diane lifted her face mask, her disappointment clear. "Ah, Daddy, can't we do it just a little longer?"

"I think that's enough for today," he stated, bending to remove his fins.

"Please!" Diane begged. "I can do it by myself. It was easy."

"Diane..." Maxwell began in a warning voice. Eva watched the exchange anxiously.

Seeing that her father meant it, Diane pouted and began to angrily pull her mask off.

"Now just a minute," Adam began sternly. "Don't try a temper tantrum with me. I said that's enough for the first time. You can try it again tomorrow. Okay?"

"Yes..." Diane whispered, her stubborn disappointment warring against her quivering emotions at being disciplined again. Maxwell turned from Diane to Eva who stood watching the episode with a quiet sympathetic frown for both of them on her soft brown face.

Maxwell's face went from sternness to impatience. He looked at Eva silently for a moment and turned back to his daughter, still standing dejectedly behind him.

"Look...I'll let you practice another half hour..."

Immediately Diane came to life, her eyes lighting up in a smile.

"But I want you right here where I can keep an eye on you."

"Thanks, Daddy," she gushed, pulling the mask on again and untwisting a side bun and setting the thick strands of hair free.

"Wait. I'm not finished yet."

Diane's smile faded as she recognized the hard command in her father's voice. But surprisingly Maxwell gentled his tone, or at least as much as his deep voice would allow.

"I don't want any more pouting from you when I say no. And the next time I say no, I mean it. Understand?"

She kept her head down.

"Look at me. Do you understand?"

"Yes..." she responded, no longer piqued, but looking seriously at her father as someone who would, indeed, not brook any more nonsense from her. Maxwell stood with his hands braced on his hips.

"And when I say it's time to come out, I won't hear any more complaining, right?"

"Yes, Daddy."

"All right." He nodded, dismissing her, and quietly Diane went back into the water.

Eva was impressed. It was the most effective handling of Diane she'd seen Maxwell perform. Eva realized that both father and daughter had so much to learn about each other. It was also clear that Diane tried to manipulate her father to get her way, as children will, but Maxwell dealt with it firmly and constructively.

Maxwell now stood looking at her strangely. Eva felt self-conscious again and looked around hastily for her cover-up.

"Forget it," Maxwell declared, reading her mind. "You won't be needing it." He reached toward her and took her by the arm. "Come on...it's time you learned how to swim."

"Now just a minute!" Eva said haughtily, pulling her arm. "You can't treat me as if I'm your daughter." But her argument was as ineffective as Diane's had been.

"I don't think I'm likely to make that mistake," he drawled suggestively, sweeping his eyes over her attractive frame. That completely silenced her. Whether or not it was meant as a compliment, she didn't know how to handle it. She was led into the water, and already Maxwell was talking to her about what to do with her arms and legs. He treated her rather impersonally, and that made it easier for her to listen and follow his actions. She forgot about being self-conscious in the tangerine suit that so clearly outlined all her curves. But she still could not control the odd tremor that seemed inevitable each time Maxwell came too close.

His giant hands circled her waist, touched her arms and legs. He floated her on her back, supporting her with a hand intimately on her buttocks, the other hand at her neck.

"Now put your head way back…relax, Eva, I'm not going to let you go," he assured her.

Eva's hair floated out from her head like a short dark fan as her head went farther back in the water.

"Use your stomach muscles…that's it! Pull in, and push out your chest." The hand from her bottom moved to rest gently on her stomach, spanning the whole surface and then moving over the wet suit to her rib cage. Eva drew in a breath sharply in awareness of the stroking.

"Good!" Maxwell approved her action, not knowing the real cause. "Just relax."

The sun was toasty warm on her face. She felt wonderfully free and alive. A smile curved her mouth, and she could not see, with her eyes closed against the overhead brilliance of the sun, Adam watching her with a thoughtful expression on his face.

"You're doing fine," he said vaguely, distantly to her ears. He seemed too far away. Eva opened her eyes and didn't see Maxwell anywhere in her line of vision. She lost her poise and confidence and her position and sank beneath the water.

At once Eva felt strong hands pull her up by the waist, and she was hauled against Maxwell's warm chest. She came up laughing.

"You okay?" Maxwell asked with no concern.

"Yes," Eva answered, finding her footing in the sandy bottom. Only then as she stood on her own was she conscious that Maxwell held her rather closely. Too closely. Her hands were braced against his chest. Her head barely reached his shoulders. He seemed much larger than she first realized. His thighs pressed against hers were rough with hair and incredibly taut.

Slowly Eva raised her eyes to look into his face. She was certain that Maxwell had a kind of permanent hard fixture to his rugged face, always making him look forbidding. But his eyes were different. The light brown of them was bright, searching…and soft. There was a new interest in them, making Eva aware of her femininity and his maleness. Her heart began beating faster as Maxwell raised a hand to her neck and barely touching the skin slid his fingers up the side to her jaw. Eva began pushing away from him. In the next instant they were totally jerked apart by the frantic cry of Diane out in the bay.

Chapter Four

Maxwell pushed Eva and released her so abruptly that she fell into the surf up to her neck. But already Maxwell had cleaved the surface of the water cleanly and with long powerful strokes started for Diane. Diane was a good swimmer, and Eva was, therefore, confused as to what had gone wrong. The little girl was farther away from shore than she should have been. She was sputtering water and obviously in trouble.

Adam was moving very fast, but it seemed an eternity before he reached Diane, her body now frighteningly limp, and started back to shore with her. Eva found a towel and held it ready to wrap around her wet body when she reached the beach.

Maxwell carried Diane from the water, his mouth and eyes grim and sternly set. Eva gasped, her hand flying to her mouth in dread when it appeared that Diane was unconscious. She stood stunned as Maxwell lowered her to the sand, yanking off the face mask and hose and tossing it aside. At once he pushed Diane's head back until her chin was straight up and, covering the child's mouth with his own, began to blow air rapidly into her lungs. Then he flipped her over on her stomach and pushed the heel of his hand roughly into her back between her shoulder blades. Diane coughed once, water gushing from her mouth. Again Adam placed her on her back. But before he could again breathe into her mouth, she coughed again, and her eyes fluttered open. Maxwell pulled her into a sitting position. Suddenly Diane heaved and, holding her head down, Maxwell let her lose her lunch and all the salt water she'd swallowed as well. At last Eva came alert and hurried over to wipe Diane's damp face and put the towel around her chest.

Diane looked at her father's face, finally focusing on him. Her face collapsed and she began to cry.

"Daddy!" she screamed in awful fright and threw herself against her father's chest. Maxwell's jaw clenched, and he held his daughter so tightly that Eva was afraid he'd hurt her.

Eva's heart turned over when Maxwell lifted his eyes to her with a tortured expression on his face as he realized the near tragedy they'd escaped. He didn't seem capable of words in that moment, and Eva understood. She herself got up and quickly gathered the things scattered in the sand around them. And while Adam continued to hold, rock, and comfort the frightened little girl, Eva put everything into the launch. Finally Maxwell attempted to get Diane to her feet, but she moaned and fell back to her knees.

"Ooooooh! It hurts…it hurts!" she whimpered. Adam looked at her feet and, lifting her once more into his arms, moved with her to the waiting launch. Eva climbed in first and sat with her arms held open. Adam placed Diane next to her, and immediately Eva's arms closed around Diane, who put her head to Eva's chest and quietly sobbed.

There had been no time to put on her cover-up, and her skin was now raised with gooseflesh as the cool sea breeze touched her still-wet skin. Diane was sick again and Eva let her relieve herself in the end of the towel then once again wiped her mouth clean.

In the meantime Maxwell was silent, fast, and efficient. In no time he had them back on the sailing vessel, and the launch was secured to a trail line behind the craft. He went below deck and came back with a bottle of vinegar. Eva frowned at him as he lifted Diane's left foot. For the first time Eva could see that the foot was slightly swollen and there was a large red spot on the underside. She was even more confused when Maxwell poured generous amounts on the small puncture in the skin, and Diane winced in pain, clutching at Eva and beginning to cry again.

Maxwell met Eva's concerned gaze.

"She stepped on a sea urchin," he mumbled. "The acid in the vinegar will dissolve any particles left in her foot. It'll hurt like hell for a day or so, but she'll be okay."

"Are you sure?" Eva asked softly, pulling the little girl to her, resting her chin against Diane's hair. Maxwell looked at his daughter, his expression still anguished and tight.

"She just had a bad scare. But she'll be fine."

Then he stood and left them, preparing once more to put the vessel under sail and return them home to Hawksnest Bay.

The trip back seemed to take a long time, but finally they were back. Eva let out a sigh of relief. Diane was much calmer now, but still whimpering with the returning memory of her ordeal and the throbbing in her left foot. Maxwell managed to get Diane into the launch, Eva following on her own, and it was a rather silent, shocked trio that reached the beach.

"I'll come with you," Eva stated, as Maxwell carried Diane to the Jeep. He merely nodded in agreement. At last Eva was able to put on her damp and very wrinkled cover-up. She climbed into the back seat of the Jeep. When they arrived at the house, Eva turned to Maxwell.

"Why don't I get her cleaned up and in bed first. Then you can come in and see her."

Maxwell hesitated.

"I'll only be ten minutes. I'll just get the sand and salt water off her and fix her hair."

He finally nodded, and Eva helped Diane off to the bathroom. Silently he turned to unload the Jeep. He'd just finished hosing off the last of the snorkel gear when Eva came up behind him in the front yard.

"Maxwell..." She touched the hard sinewed back. Adam turned around, frowning. "She's in bed. You can go in now. You were right. Her foot hurts, but she was just scared."

Maxwell moved to brush past her, and Eva put a restraining hand on his arm.

"Maxwell..."

He stopped to look down at her in the fading light of dusk. Eva hesitated, not wanting to seem as interfering or to preach and sound pompous, but very much wanting to ease the way for both father and daughter.

"She thinks you're going to be mad at her. That's bothering her more than anything."

He remained silent and stone-still. Eva drew in a deep breath.

"Please don't yell at her tonight..."

He stared at her a moment longer, then abruptly, without responding, he moved around her into the house, leaving Eva looking anxiously at his retreating form. Eva hugged herself in the sudden cool air. Staring out over the low-topped trees, she watched the purple sunset on the horizon, watching the sky get darker and darker. It had been a horribly frightening moment this afternoon when Adam had rushed out of the water with Diane in his arms.

Eva remembered when Gail was five and had fallen from a tricycle, putting a serious gash in her forehead and abrasions on her knees. Eva had been beside herself with panic that some more serious internal head injury had occurred. Later in the emergency room, Kevin had told her with a rueful smile that their daughter's biggest concern was all the blood that now stained her new blue jump suit. Of course, that incident had paled to total insignificance with the fire years later.

Eva turned and walked slowly into the house. She vaguely registered that it was much neater this time than the first time she'd been here. But the books, papers, samples, and journals lay pretty much as before. Eva heard the soft low voices behind Diane's closed bedroom door. The deeper, richer sound of Maxwell, and the softer, higher one of Diane. Suddenly there was a giggle and a brief rough chuckle from Maxwell. Smiling to herself and relaxing, Eva began to dig through the refrigerator and cupboards, looking for something to fix to eat. It was nearly an hour later before she heard Diane's door open and close. Eva went to the square opening connecting the roof deck and lower rooms.

"Maxwell!" she whispered loudly. "I'm up here."

Eva heard his footsteps. Then he stood under the opening, peering up at her dark form silhouetted against the night sky.

"What are you doing up there?" he questioned.

"I thought you could use something to eat."

He came up the ladder, still wearing his swim trunks

and now, also, a light-blue work shirt, unbuttoned half down his chest. Eva gestured to the small round table that contained a plate with cold chicken, bean salad, and slices of onion bread. She picked up a glass and gave it to him.

"And I thought you could use a stiff drink." She grinned, making note of the look of appreciation on his face. He looked exhausted. Maxwell sighed, took the glass, and emptied it in two gulps. He tried to hold back a cough but couldn't, as the liquid burned its way down his throat.

"That's straight rum!" he rasped out in his deep voice.

"That's right." Eva smiled. Maxwell looked thoughtfully at the empty glass before setting it on the table.

"I swear kids can drive you to drink," he commented to her dryly.

Eva chuckled lightly. "Yes, I know." Maxwell did not follow up by asking her how she knew, and she didn't think to enlighten him. Eva got him to sit down and watched as he absently began to eat. He didn't thank her for the food and didn't comment on it. He was deep in thought, and Eva left him to his own inner workings as his brows furrowed in some concentration. He was completely finished eating before he said anything at all. He looked up at her.

"You didn't eat anything. Are you on a diet?"

Eva smiled in the dark, shaking her head. "Are you suggesting I need to lose weight?" she asked.

"I'm not suggesting anything," he said wearily, running a hand across the back of his neck. "I was just asking a civil question. That's all."

"Well then, I guess I'm surprised at your concern," Eva said smoothly, without rancor.

She could see Maxwell's head slowly lift in her direction again, searching for her eyes and expression.

"You don't think very much of me, do you?" he asked conversationally, but not as if he really cared one way or another. Eva settled back farther into her chair.

"I think it's more the other way around. You don't really care for me…"

"It's not you…"

"Okay…women in general then. Except for Lavona Morris, of course. She has obviously found the way to your…heart."

"You don't know anything about Lavona and me."

Eva laughed softly in real amusement, sure of herself. "Maxwell…I know everything about it!"

"You know nothing!" he grounded out hard. His vehemence surprised Eva. "You think I'm conducting an affair with her right here in this house under my daughter's nose!"

"Well, aren't you?" Eva accused.

Maxwell chuckled dryly. "I was right. You don't think very much of me." He stood up and walked to the edge of the deck, bracing his hands on the railing. "I told you once before this isn't a very large island. But still there are a dozen places I can go to be alone…or with Lavona. I don't have to do that in Diane's presence." But he didn't deny that he was having an affair with Lavona.

Eva was quiet for a moment, realizing that she was way out of line. "I'm sorry," she said low. "It's not my business…and I shouldn't criticize."

"But you still don't like the idea."

"Maxwell…my concern is for Diane. It must confuse her, seeing you with Lavona. And I don't think Diane likes her very much. Maybe she feels…threatened."

"That's stupid," he growled impatiently.

"Not to a ten-year-old child who once a year had to start all over again getting close to her father. Maxwell, she's just not sure where she stands with you."

"But I'm her father!"

"Yes! But do you treat her like she's your daughter?" Eva asked forcefully. They stood tense and indignant, and, Eva at least, unsure. She sighed. "There I go again."

She was surprised at the sarcasm in Maxwell's voice when he spoke again. "I guess she's lucky to have you on her side. Under different circumstances you'd make a great lawyer." He turned away to look out into the night.

"What other circumstances?" Eva frowned.

Maxwell remained silent for a very long time. Then he turned around, bracing himself against the railing and crossing his powerful arms over his chest. "Other times, when you're not busy being maternal and domestic…fussing over Diane. Cleaning up houses."

"You make it sound like some kind of—of disease I have," she said in amazement. "I thought I was just being concerned and helpful. Would you have preferred if I'd stood around and just watched?"

"I don't think you can help all those instincts," Maxwell explained. "You need to feel you're important to someone."

Eva just stared at him wide-eyed. "Why, you conceited…I'm an independent human being, Maxwell, but does that mean I shouldn't care? Why are the two terms mutually exclusive in your mind?" she asked angrily.

"I really doubt that women want to be independent. You'll play at being alone and running your own lives, but the bottom line is you're all looking for someone to take care of you."

"That's insulting." Eva stood up indignantly. "You have no right to say that to me!"

"And how dare you presume to tell me how to raise my child! What do you know about being a parent!" he bit out angrily. He'd hit a sore nerve and Eva was silent, grabbing for the edge of the table. Her hands were shaking, and her heart leaped.

"It was honest concern. I—I wasn't trying to interfere," Eva said stiffly.

"You lost one husband. But you're young. You're healthy and attractive. You'll want someone else, all right..."

"Will you stop it!"

"When the fun and novelty wears off and you find you don't want to be alone, that you want a home and children."

"Don't you think you're going a bit overboard?" Eva asked, stunned.

"And then when the man's not everything you want him to be, you give up on him. Make him leave...go looking for someone else."

Eva was shocked into growing anger, her knees so weak she sat down again.

"Is that what your wife did to you?"

Maxwell stared at her silently. "What?" He frowned, puzzled now.

"You heard me. It's your ego that's hurt, Maxwell...not your sensibilities, because you haven't any!" Eva shot at him. She began to climb down the ladder back into the house. She was surprised when Maxwell followed her and grabbed her by the arm, swinging her roughly around to face him. Eva jerked away from his hold.

"Let me go!"

"I want to know what you meant?"

"No, you don't! You couldn't care less what I say or what I mean!"

Adam took her by the arms again and shook her. "Answer me!"

"You're crazy!" she gritted out through clenched teeth. "I don't have to put up with this!" Eva pulled away again. "And apparently your poor wife felt the same way."

Maxwell stood watching her strangely, as if she'd just said something he hadn't considered before. For that matter, he looked as if he'd just been kicked in the stomach. Eva's expression in watching him slowly changed from anger to one of curiosity. Her own anger then died in the face of this metamorphosis Maxwell went through. Where had she hit on the truth that now had this man, this impregnable stone giant of a man, in the grips of some past pain?

"Maxwell?" Eva questioned as he stood in a slightly dazed state. He slowly walked away from her toward the door. He stood blocking the entrance.

"Maxwell?" Eva tried again, curious as to his sudden quietness. He turned then to regard her, his face closed, the nighttime beginnings of his beard darkening the lower part of his cheeks and chin. He looked almost evil and very menacing. His eyes swept over Eva from head to toe and back to her eyes to hold their steady gaze for long moments. His jaw worked tensely, and even as he stared at her for so long, Eva knew he wasn't seeing her at all. Suddenly he blinked rapidly as though to clear his vision and his thoughts.

"I don't expect anything more from Lavona Morris than what she gives. And she gives that freely...and frequently." He showed no guilt or remorse at the admission. But then again, why should he?

"And what does she get from you?" Eva asked quietly.

Maxwell's frown deepened, as the question sank in. "The same thing, I suppose. But nothing more."

Maxwell suddenly opened the door. He looked back over his shoulder at Eva. "But my wife—my wife is a different story." But he didn't say how. "Come on. I'll take you back to your house." He continued through the door without looking back or waiting for her to respond.

Eva hurried to catch up to him. "You don't have to. I'm perfectly capable of going home alone," Eva stated firmly. "Despite your opinion of me, I'm not helpless."

His sudden remoteness indicated a number of things to Eva that she recognized at once: exhaustion, both physical and emotional after the day's adventure, and a thoughtfulness that she was sure had to do with mentioning his ex-wife. His verbal attack on her she felt was unnecessary, but it was obvious that she'd held up better under fire than he did.

"Whether you're helpless or not isn't the issue. It's very dark and the road is unfamiliar to you. I'm taking you home!"

There was a definite finality to his tone that Eva gave in to. She had nothing to gain with further arguments.

They first had to get her Jeep from where it was left earlier in the day on the beach. In the darkness they walked along the uneven rocky road in silence. Eva found the quiet between them depressing and unbearable, but she couldn't think of a single thing to say. She stumbled in the dark and gasped, reaching out her hand for balance. At once Maxwell reached out to steady her, his hand moving along her arm and finally grabbing her hand strongly. He continued to hold it securely to lead her, but it was totally impersonal and only meant as a gesture for safety's sake. Eva was nonetheless glad for his support when she tripped a second time before reaching the Jeep, which was pulled over on the side of the road.

"I'll drive," he said releasing her hand and getting behind the driver's seat.

"How will you get back home?" Eva questioned.

Maxwell put the key in the ignition and started the engine. "It's only a half mile. I can walk it in ten or fifteen minutes. Get in."

They continued in silence all the way to Eva's house, and Maxwell followed her up the cement steps from the driveway, through the gate, and into the gallery. He put her tote on the floor.

"I don't want to leave Diane too long…in case she wakes up in pain," he said in his deep voice.

Eva nodded. "I understand. I—I'm sorry I wasn't more help this afternoon."

"You did okay," Maxwell said, leaning casually against a support column. He looked at her in a certain searching way that made Eva feel very exposed and open to his gaze. Suddenly Maxwell shook his head, closed his eyes, and passed a hand across his bristled cheek and then over the back of his neck.

"What made you think I was going to yell at her?" he asked.

Eva frowned. "What?"

"When we got home with Diane. You told me not to yell at her tonight. What made you think that I would?"

Eva hesitated, watching the tired man in front of her. He didn't hold much tolerance for her interference earlier, and she wasn't sure he'd appreciate it any better now. She shrugged. "I don't know. You seem…so impatient with her. She's curious and quick, and she gets into a lot of things you don't want her to. But she's just being a child. She needs time…and patience,'' Eva ended softly.

Maxwell watched her for a long moment, his jaw working, his eyes narrowing at her. Eva prepared herself for another tirade.

"I guess I'm a lousy excuse for a father. I always seem to do or say the wrong thing to her."

Eva was surprised and instantly moved by this confession. "Oh, Maxwell…you're not a—a bad father.''

"I don't know how to handle her,'' he said in some frustration, swinging a hand in gesture. Eva smiled at the motion of helplessness.

"She doesn't need handling,'' Eva suggested softly. Maxwell glowered at her in his usual manner, but there was, nonetheless, an expectant expression in his eyes as he stared at her. "I think what Diane needs is to know you love her and that you really want her here with you.''

He stared down now at his sandals. Eva had never seen him so unsure of himself. This made her smile, too. She walked over to him and laid a soft, small hand on his forearm. She felt the muscles tighten in response under her fingers.

"You haven't had a chance to be a father. You just lack some experience is all."

Maxwell made a soundless chuckle. "It's hard to be a father long distance."

Eva bit her lip. He sounded bitter, making her curious again about his ex-wife. "There is the rest of her vacation…"

"And what do I do when the vacation is over? Send her back to New York and let her mother wipe me from her memory again with her bad mouthing and put-downs?''

"You don't know that she does that. And you can't

blame your wife forever. If you knew Diane better, you'd know that no one can damage your image in her eyes, except you. She's old enough to understand her separations from you. You just keep letting her know how important she is to you.''

Eva's voice broke, and she felt a wave of emotion wash over her. She missed Gail. She missed her own pretty little girl who would have been almost a full year older than Diane Maxwell. Maxwell had his daughter here with him. He could love her and help her to grow into a lovely, happy young woman. Eva couldn't bear it if he lost that chance and lost his child as well.

They were both tired and both high-strung from the emotional impact of the day, and in each of their hearts Eva knew it was for the same reasons.

She clutched at Maxwell's arm, and somehow, she was never to know how, they were locked in each other's embrace. Her head was pressed against his hard warm chest, the hair through the open front of his shirt surprisingly soft on her cheek. She rubbed her face against it, closing her eyes. A deep sigh of comfort escaped her as Maxwell's arms tightened. The whole solid length of him was hard against her. It was like being embraced by a bear.

Eva didn't question for one moment his holding her. She had instantly tapped into the Maxwell that was a questioning, uncertain parent, rather than the hard, uncompromising man. They were not antagonists now, and there was a momentary mutual sympathy.

Eva recognized in him the confusion and possible fears of being just a part-time father, of being responsible for another life and not sure you're doing everything right. And although Maxwell couldn't have known it, Eva needed comforting against the sudden onslaught of her past grief. If it had to be anyone to die, why couldn't it have been she and not Gail? The warm embrace held them each together, kept them whole, gave them some kind of strength to go on. Neither had asked for this, but here it was. And then it changed.

Maxwell's hand came up to cup and caress her cheek, his thumb firmly pushing her chin up, tilting her head back so he could see her face. He was as close now as he'd been this afternoon when he began to teach her to swim, but his look was altogether different. Eva was aware of his brown rugged features, his firm square chin lowering toward her. His mouth was pressed to hers and rested there. It was nice. It was easy. Just another comforting gesture she didn't know he was capable of.

But then his mouth moved, caressing the full surface of her lips, pulling on them, his tongue quickly moistening the curves before they separated involuntarily. Eva's eyes flew wide open in complete surprise. They searched his hard face to find his eyes watching her mouth, his jaw tensing.

"Max?" she whispered in confusion, shortening his name to something special. He quirked a corner of his mouth at her, as his forefinger gently outlined her lips.

"When you kiss a man, it's okay to call him by his first name..." he actually teased. Before she could change her bewildered expression, he had gathered her once more against him and began to kiss her in earnest. His wide, well-shaped mouth coaxed her lips apart, and his warm tongue furrowed deep inside to stroke against her own. Eva's mind spun around dizzily. Maxwell was very slow and excruciatingly deliberate in his exploration, and all of Eva's senses were zeroed in to the feel of his mouth over hers. It held her rigid...and fascinated.

She had grown to adulthood only knowing one man's

kisses, one man's touch. It had been very pleasant and warm. She'd enjoyed being held and loved by Kevin Duncan. But her relationship to her husband was all she had to compare this new embrace to. Something told her this was wrong. She shouldn't be feeling this way, as if her legs were limp noodles and her mind was bursting with wild bright colors. She shouldn't be so pliant and yielding, letting another man have his way. She shouldn't be feeling that if he didn't stop for a long, long time she wouldn't care. She shouldn't be responding, enjoying it, melting into him, giving him complete access to her mouth. It was a gentle sensuous caressing, the kiss deepening even more. She had no clear thought of holding back, of not participating. His one hand around her shoulders, alternately massaged and pressed her nearer. That was one thing. But when Maxwell's other hand made a sensuous journey up the back of one thigh causing a quaking through the center of her body as he pressed her buttocks to bring her against his distinct hard masculine form, she finally came to her senses, pulling her mouth away with a gasp and turning completely within the circle of his arms.

"No! Please, Maxwell...don't!" she breathed erratically. His arms remained around her, holding her to him. Against her back Eva could feel the pounding of his heart, his quickened breathing over the top of her head, the length of him hot against her back. And there was no mistaking the changing feel of him now.

Eva pulled loose and walked unsteadily away from him. But now she was too ashamed to turn around and face him. And she didn't want him to say anything, afraid of his sarcasm.

"I'm sorry," Maxwell said very low, breathing out, his deep voice a bass rumbling through the silence of the open gallery. Eva heard him, heard the words, and slowly shook her head.

"No you're not," she whispered almost in pain. Her eyes were closed tightly, blocking him out deliberately. There was a quiet behind her.

"You're right...I'm not," he admitted in the same voice, same tone.

How could she expect him to be sorry when, if the truth were known, she wasn't sorry either? She was only very scared.

When Eva turned around finally, Adam Maxwell was gone, and she stood in the open gallery all alone.

Eva felt unreal. Suspended. An unmistakable terror took hold of her as she slowly walked into the bedroom. A chill swept over her, raising bumps on her flesh. She hugged herself. She realized that there was a part of her that had enjoyed thoroughly Maxwell's kissing her, squeezing her soft frame to his harder one. She had acquiesced to his mouth drawing a response from her own.

Eva moved in front of the mirror over a low dresser. She looked the same. Maybe her eyes were a little bright and startled-looking. Maybe her lips were still moist and parted, kissed into softness. She raised her right hand with a slight tremor to her cheek. Maybe the skin was a little warm and sensitive with emotion. But she looked the same.

Eva lowered her hand and eyes from her image with infinite sadness and silently shook her head. She was not the same. And beyond a doubt she knew she would never be again.

Eva gently twisted off Kevin Duncan's wedding band. The shiny gold was almost instantly cold in her hand. She looked at it long and hard. Tears blinded her vision, making the gold shimmer, before rolling down her cheeks. Eva tied the ring into a linen handkerchief and placed it in a zippered compartment in her suitcase.

IT WAS another perfect day on the island. Eva rose early and dressed in a white summer sun dress with thin spaghetti straps. It buttoned down the front all the way to the hem of its A-line skirt and had two pockets constructed of lacy Irish linen handkerchiefs. The white of the dress was startling and very pretty against her brown skin.

She wasn't going to the beach today. Sitting there and speculating would add nothing to her already shaken state of mind. She hadn't slept well the night before, but she had no intention of making more of last night's encounter with Adam Maxwell than was actually there. In the clear light of day, she saw it as a spontaneous happening. She was sure of it. But last night, in the dark all alone, that belief had not been present.

For a long time she could think and feel nothing but the pressure of his mouth on hers, of his weight and form against hers. There had been the smell of him, the feel of him, overwhelming, powerful and enticing all around her. Eva had felt very safe in Maxwell's arms, and she had no right to feel that way. She'd stood shaking like a leaf long after he'd gone, feeling her insides releasing themselves slowly from emotional tension so that she could move at last and sit down.

And somewhere else in her mind Kevin Duncan stood watching her in pained curiosity, watching his wife being kissed and held by another man. The guilt had sent Eva off to the shower, to wash away the feel and memory of Adam Maxwell from her skin and her mind. But he had stayed with her far into the night, until mourning doves set up a repetitive cooing with the coming daylight, and she moaned awake, utterly exhausted.

Today she would go back to St. Thomas and spend the day involved in something else. She'd treat herself to lunch and maybe shop for gifts and souvenirs. She'd walk until she was too tired to think and then maybe tonight she'd sleep. But she had one thing to do first.

Eva left her house and purposefully drove the half mile to Adam Maxwell's. It was a little after ten o'clock, and she'd planned her time so that she could check in on Diane, say hello, and leave reasonably soon to catch the eleven o'clock ferry. This way she could not later be accused by Maxwell of deliberately avoiding him all day.

Eva left the Jeep on the road and climbed the short incline in her low-heeled sandals to the door. She knocked and waited, concentrating on staying calm and settling the sudden swarm of butterflies in her stomach. She was totally nonplussed when the door opened and a doe-eyed Lavona Morris stood there. Eva knew she must have gaped with her mouth open, and she quickly closed it.

Lavona never said a word but lounged rather indolently against the door frame as if she belonged there. She cast a heavy-lidded, haughty look over Eva in a none-too-complimentary way. It succeeded in momentarily unnerving Eva, making her more than conscious of Lavona's obvious feminine appeal. And she made it obvious that she had no intention of making Eva feel welcomed.

"I—I came to see how Diane was doing today. She had an accident yesterday."

Lavona smiled only slightly, raising her chin. "Adam say so." Her tongue moved slowly around the name, saying it with two distinct syllables, her musical island accent only making the words sound lightly foreign. Eva couldn't help being fascinated with Lavona's speech pattern. It was lovely.

"How is she?" Eva inquired, knowing that Lavona was not about to let her into the house to see for herself. Eva felt powerless to force the issue.

Lavona shrugged a smooth round shoulder. "She is asleep now," she answered with a noticeable lack of concern. She was dressed in a calico-print summer dress of a lightweight fabric. It was belted at the waist and clung in the moist heat to her womanly form.

Eva took a deep breath and forged on. "Is her foot any better today?"

"It's only tunchy bite, you know. Not too bad."

Eva nodded vaguely, not sure of all she heard. She wondered if Diane thought it was "not too bad." Children's pain was usually a little more substantial than that. Eva couldn't think of what else to say as she stood feeling foolish in front of Lavona.

"Adam won't come back for a time," Lavona volunteered. Eva wasn't going to ask where he was, but now she at least knew he wasn't here with Lavona. Eva chose to pretend it wasn't important.

"Could you please just tell Diane that Eva was here? Tell her I went into St. Thomas, and I hope she's feeling better."

Lavona nodded once, but Eva wasn't all that sure that Diane would get the whole message.

"Tell her I'll visit another time."

"I'll tell her," Lavona agreed. And if Eva had anything else to say, it was just too bad since the door was then quietly closed on her.

Eva felt anger welling up in her. Lavona's attitude had been unbearable. And if it wasn't for a genuine liking and concern for Diane, she'd never come near this house again.

Turning away, Eva climbed into her Jeep and leisurely made her way into Cruz Bay to await the next ferry. She had no trouble whatsoever reversing her steps into Charlotte Amalie, and arrived feeling rather pleased with herself.

Adam Maxwell might not think her independent, but he had no idea of the things she'd accomplished in the last two years of living almost on her own. It was true that her mother had insisted she move back home after she'd recovered from her personal shock, but she'd found the adage about never going home again true. She wanted and needed to establish her own place.

For the almost nine years that she'd been married, Eva remained home, running the house and raising a daughter. She married Kevin right after high school, and it wasn't until after she was totally on her own again that she'd taken a year's certificate program at a local college, worked part-time, and thought of continuing college until she was qualified for a more demanding and interesting job. A person does what he or she has to do. She'd needed to prove she could take care of herself, take responsibility for her own life again.

Eva resisted the urge to buy a map and armed with her camera and sunglasses, started from the farthest end of Charlotte Amalie, behind the Windward Passage Hotel, and slowly worked her way up the narrow cobbled streets. Old Dutch fort buildings had been converted into large open-air shops, peopled by local native citizens selling a variety of imported European goods, as well as the work of local artisans.

Eva passed the Market Square, obviously used for the exchange and purchasing of fresh produce and dry goods.

But today it was virtually empty except for a number of elderly citizens taking the afternoon sun and chatting among themselves. Eva took a number of pictures, wishing she could also capture on film the musical language. There were a number of narrow alleyways between Waterfront Highway and the main street with such names as Cutter's Gade, International Plaza, Palm Passage, and Creque's Alley West. In these passages were modern gift shops and cafés, small gardens, and fountains.

Eva spent a leisurely time exploring the streets, ignoring the occasional catcalls from the local men coming on to a lone, young, attractive woman. But Eva was not flattered by the attention. It made her feel vulnerable and very unprepared. She'd never had anyone whistle after her in her life. It was definitely a unique experience.

She passed a shop of beautifully hand-batiked cloth and wandered inside with the intention of purchasing a length of fabric for her mother and sisters-in-law. A friendly, soft-spoken saleswoman showed her around the bright, pleasant shop.

Two young women, apparent tourists, were trying on lengths of fabric that were wrapped artfully around their thin, curvy bodies and secured by merely twisting and tucking the ends. Eva watched in curiosity. The finished garment looked pretty, comfortable, and alluring.

"Would you like to try one?" the saleslady asked.

"Oh no!" Eva laughed. "I couldn't wear that! Where would I wear it?" she ended with a question. Perhaps the saleslady sensed she only needed a little persuasion.

"Women all the time wear them here. Around the house, to a picnic or the beach. You wear to dance for your man, yes?" and then she laughed softly. She led a non-resisting Eva to a dressing room. "You try on. Very pretty on you."

Eva was passed a piece of pale blue cloth batiked with flowers in different shades of yellow. She held it up skeptically, not believing there was enough cloth here to keep her decently covered. But she wrapped it around and the saleslady showed her how to secure it. And it stayed.

Eva was entranced by her changed appearance in front of a mirror. Her upper chest and shoulders were bare, but with her slender neck exposed by her short haircut, she was very surprised and pleased with the results. Chuckling nonetheless at the absurdity of it, Eva bought the java wrap, as it was called. She continued on her walk, reaching Creque's Alley West by two o'clock in the afternoon. On impulse she purchased a pair of cute hair barrettes and a few children's paperback books for Diane, thinking they would cheer her up. Then Eva stopped into L'Escargot restaurant and enjoyed a leisurely late lunch, people-watching and deciding on how to spend the rest of the day.

For a time she walked along the dock front, taking pictures of the fishing boats and the impromptu stands where women and men sold fruit and vegetables such as yucca, mangoes, plantines, and sugar cane. The sun was shifting, starting its descent, and Eva was just thinking of taking a cab back to the ferry when she reached into her purse to discover her wallet was missing. Frantically she dug among the few things in her bag, but it wasn't there. Luckily she still had her traveler's checks, but the banks and stores were closed now and there was no place to cash one. In her mind she backtracked over the day, thinking that perhaps she'd left it somewhere. But she'd stopped at more than a dozen places, even arranging at one or two for things to be shipped back to the States. Eva gave up the attempt. Her only consolation was that there was only about twenty dollars in cash in the wallet and her driver's license. But the money would have paid for a return taxi to Red Hook and the ferry ride back to Cruz Bay.

Eva decided that the best thing to do was to walk the quarter mile or so to the police station and explain her situation. She was just a little past the post office when a car pulled up beside her.

"Taxi, lady?" a voice asked.

Eva didn't turn her head. "No, thank you," she said firmly, hoping she didn't have much farther to go, as it was already getting dark.

"Why you don't let Deacon take you 'roun the island?"

Eva stopped and looked into a familiar, smiling face. "Oh! Hello!"

"Hello, lady. I told you you come back to St. Thomas. Why you not look up Deacon, eh?"

Eva laughed. "I—I forgot," she said. "How did you know it was me?" she now asked.

He laughed. "Oh, Deacon always remember a pretty face. Where you go now? Not back to St. John yet?"

Eva smiled in wry amusement. "Maybe not tonight at all! I lost my wallet somewhere with my money. I was just on my way to the police…"

"Oh, you lucky lady. You don't need police…you have Deacon!"

"You don't have to bother," Eva said. "I'm sure the police will arrange something."

Deacon finally stepped out of the cab and stood in front of Eva with his indomitable smile on his dark face. He was only a few inches taller than Eva and fidgeted somewhat shyly in front of her.

"I tell you what…there's a bit of light left. I take you round St. Thomas fast. We go to Mountain Top and you taste daiquiris. St. Thomas very famous for rum drinks..."

"But...I don't really drink," Eva tried to dissuade him. He was not discouraged and scoffed cheerfully at her.

"Daiquiri very sweet drink, just for ladies. Perfect for you, yes?"

When Eva tried to object again, he quietly raised a hand to silence her.

"Then I take you to best place for island food. Afterward...if you really want, you can leave Deacon and return to St. John. My good friend Felix run ferry. He do me favor for lady."

"Eva..." Eva supplied, feeling odd just being called "lady." She felt overwhelmed. She didn't have a real reason to say no, except for an innate sense of caution that told her this man, despite his cheerfulness, was a complete stranger. It sounded like such fun, however, and after all, what were the immediate alternatives? The police station or checking into a hotel overnight. And she admitted she was not looking forward to dinner alone. This was her vacation, and she'd come to have a good time. So, why not?

Deacon could probably see her resistance giving way, because he began to laugh softly and to nod in satisfaction.

"All right...I'll come." Eva gave in, with just a trace of lingering hesitation. Deacon completely dispelled that last bit when he simply reached for her hand to formally shake it.

"Good. You have good time! My name Deacon Butler, and I work for this company..." He pointed to the name carved in white letters on the side of the cab door. "And if anything go wrong, you call them. They get after Deacon, fast!''

"And I'm Eva Duncan," Eva said, accepting the hand he offered. She had to admit that it was kind of exciting to be on speaking terms with someone who lived here. She felt she'd gone a little beyond the realm of being just a tourist.

Deacon Butler became the perfect gentleman, seating Eva next to him in the front of the cab, and cheerfully talking as he turned the car in another direction and began a climb into the mountainside overlooking Charlotte Amalie. At last they reached an airy tavern with a large semicircular bar. There was a tall, gaunt island man explaining the history of daiquiris as he blended a pitcherful for his audience. He spotted Deacon and nodded in greeting without missing a step in his preparations or a beat in his anecdote. Eva was shown to an end stool, and she and Deacon had tall glasses of banana daiquiris, which Eva decided didn't taste alcoholic at all. But Deacon had to convince her that two was all she'd want.

Next he quickly circled various neighborhoods and sections of the island. As it was finally getting totally dark, they came back to Charlotte Amalie to an area known as Savan, where Deacon himself lived. In the soft quiet of the night, Deacon and Eva walked through the narrow, hilly streets of simple, unpretentious homes. Always in the background Eva was aware of the beat of music, low and rhythmic with drums. It set up a cadence that she soon became familiar with.

They stopped at a very small restaurant, again where Deacon obviously knew everyone. They were seated at a small, square Formica table. There were no tablecloths or mellow candles in the center of the table, and the napkins were paper. The silverware and plates were mismatched, but Eva relaxed entirely, knowing that she was going to experience a true part of island life…its unique and tasty cuisine.

Eva let Deacon order everything, since he assured her he knew what she'd like. While they waited for their meal, he leaned across the table to talk to her.

"So, what you think of my island, eh?"

"I think it's wonderful," Eva assured him. "It's been a lovely trip so far."

"I told you so. Island folks are nice people, yes?"

"Yes." Eva chuckled at his immodest statement. "But I don't think I could live here all the time…" Eva grimaced at him.

"Why not?"

Eva shook her head ruefully. "It would be hard to get anything done. How can anyone think of work with a beach at hand all the time?"

Deacon laughed softly in understanding. "Oh yes, you learn…or you don't eat!"

"Have you ever been to the States?"

"No. Deacon lost without island. Too fast up there. I stay here and I be happy. You stay here, you be happy all the time, too!"

"I couldn't do that."

"Oh yes. You marry Deacon, and you stay," he said, grinning.

Eva laughed at him, but she didn't know how to respond to this second suggestion that she marry him. She was beginning to think he was more than half serious. "Are you looking for a wife?"

"I look for very nice lady all the time."

"But what about all the available women right here? I'm sure there are some looking for a nice man to marry."

"Oh…I ask them, too!"

"Well, don't give up." Eva smiled positively.

"Aaaah! But I like you! You don't want to marry me and live here forever?"

Eva sighed in some exasperation at his persistence. He was rather a nice man. "I like you, too. And you're…very charming. But, I—I'm not looking for a husband."

He clicked his teeth in a sound of remorse. "That too bad. I would be very good to you!"

And Eva didn't doubt that he would be in a simple, undemanding way, probably very much like Kevin. But she didn't need that right now. Deacon, however, was not crushed by her gentle refusal.

"Maybe you change your mind. If you do, you let Deacon know, okay?"

Eva smiled warmly at him. "Okay," she said, nodding.

A number of dishes were placed before them, and Deacon began to identify and explain each one. There was one large whole red snapper that had been steamed. There was also a tureen of Kalaloo, a souplike dish with okra and conch, served with fungee balls. There were Johnny cakes, thick unleavened bread slightly sweet, and a jam made of guava to spread on it if one wanted. Yams and greens finished off the menu.

In his musical voice Deacon gave some history of the various foods to Eva, who was busy experiencing the different new tastes and textures. The little restaurant did a brisk local business, as it seemed to be busy all evening long. Everyone seemed to know everyone else, and Deacon was prompt in introducing Eva to his friends. She could never hope to remember all the names, but she was made to feel welcome.

The food and music and friendly atmosphere lulled Eva into a comfortable complacent state of being. She felt in no particular rush to get back to St. John. She felt suddenly completely her own person, capable of making her own hours. There was no one she had to answer to. It was a bittersweet realization that made her only vaguely aware of the past and only mildly curious about the future.

"You go to Carnival next week?" Deacon asked her over their warm cups of sugar tea.

Eva frowned. "What Carnival?"

"For Independence and Emancipation."

"Oh! You mean Fourth of July?"

"No...no. July third is Emancipation Day from slavery by Denmark. July fifth is Independence Day."

"Well, isn't it like July Fourth?" Eva asked, puzzled.

"Almost. But we celebrate on the islands for whole week! Lots of music, reggae, lots of food and drink. On last day there is big parade."

"It sounds like fun."

Deacon nodded. "Everyone look forward to it. You see it, too."

"Oh, I hope so! I didn't know anything about it."

"Deacon knows everything that happen here."

"I guess you do. Will you see the Carnival, too?"

"I come over one night to hear my nephew play in band. You meet me and you hear good island music."

Eva's sense of security with the man allowed her to respond with enthusiasm. "Oh, I'd love to."

"Good, good." Deacon beamed. "I come over next Thursday at six o'clock."

"I can meet you in Cruz Bay," Eva offered.

"Fine. I bring my sister and her husband. You do not mind?"

"Of course not. You can all tell me what I'm listening to."

"My nephew, Wallace, he also be Mocko Jumbi in parade on Friday."

"What's Mocko…Jumbi, is it?" Eva frowned.

"He man on long wooden legs. He like medicine man. Chase away bad spirits. Very important part of Carnival."

"I'm really looking forward to it. In the meantime I should start thinking about how I'm getting back to St. John tonight," Eva said, remembering the time. At once Deacon was solicitous and stood up.

"I take you to Red Hook. You get ferry with no trouble."

"Thank you, Deacon," Eva said sincerely, with feeling. "You've been so nice to me. I'm so glad I came to St. Thomas today."

Deacon laughed. "All nice men on St. Thomas. You come back."

"Maybe I will," she said as the bill was paid and they left the restaurant.

Eva was able to catch the nine o'clock ferry, Deacon vouching for her with his friend Felix who ran the ferry. Deacon then gallantly kissed the back of her hand and helped her board with her packages. Eva stood waving at him until he disappeared into the background of the dock in the night.

She was tired, but she felt good and soothed. However, heading back to St. John renewed the events of last night and this morning. She'd lost count of the number of times she'd relived the moment when her and Maxwell's comforting of each other turned to another kind of embrace. Eva felt curls of emotion grip at her stomach muscles every time she recalled the hard, firm fullness of Maxwell's mouth on hers. He had demonstrated an undeniable expertise in the way he'd caressed her. There was no point in trying to convince herself that it hadn't felt good. She'd been out of circulation a long time...but she wasn't dead. What she couldn't handle was his obvious arousal and his move to make the embrace more than it was. Eva couldn't believe that she had been responsible for it.

What had she done to make him want to—to touch her in that much more intimate way?

Kevin had not asked much of her in their physical relationship. She was simply supposed to be there when he needed her. She had always willingly complied. But she didn't have to do anything. Her response had merely been to acquiesce to his needs. It had been comfortable. Nothing more or less. But Maxwell had not only been much more assertive, he had expected active participation. What had also scared Eva so badly was that she wasn't sure she'd know how.

Maxwell's manliness was so overwhelming, so forceful. Here was a man who knew what he wanted and could no doubt succeed often in getting it, if Lavona Morris's presence was testimony. But he was too bold for Eva, and much too fast. She had never advanced this far in the dating game. She had never known tantalizing passions or burning desire before. Only affectionate care and gentle loving. Eva very much suspected that with Adam Maxwell she would definitely learn. But if she allowed herself to explore and find out, would she fall into an unescapable abyss that would change her whole world?

Chapter Five

Eva could see that for the second time in a row, it was going to rain all day. If she'd been on only a week's vacation, she'd be tearing her hair out and cursing the bad weather. As it was, it gave her a day and a half of time all to herself. There was time to read a book and to write out the postcards purchased on St. Thomas. But twenty-four hours of that was enough.

In the late afternoon, wearing jeans and a lightweight sweater under a foldaway rain slicker, Eva decided to go visiting. Diane was the only one likely to welcome her, and with the excuse of wanting to see how the little girl's foot was, Eva drove slowly through the drizzly miserable rain half a mile down the road.

Eva had already decided that there was also a distinct possibility that Lavona Morris would also be there, but she wasn't going to allow that to hold her back. She was mature enough to handle that situation if she had to. Maxwell could decorate his house with whomever he pleased. And Eva had so calmed down from her brief encounter with Maxwell two days earlier that there was no hesitation now as she knocked on the solid wood door. However, a moment later when Maxwell himself opened the

door, Eva jumped and just stared at his rugged good-
looking body in the doorway.

Maxwell raised a brow sardonically and waited for her
to speak first. Eva suddenly had a flash of the other night
when he'd said quite calmly that he wasn't sorry for having kissed and caressed her. Something warm and liquid
flowed through Eva, curling around in the pit of her stomach, as she recalled how she'd responded.

"Hello," Eva said politely to his imposing posture, but
he didn't respond. "I thought I'd come by and see how
Diane was doing."

Maxwell looked her over. "You didn't have to
bother," he said evenly, showing no reaction at all to her
being there. "Diane's fine now."

"I'm glad to hear it," Eva said formally, nonetheless
wondering at his stiffness and seeing that apparently
nothing had changed between them. He was still giving
her a hard time and treating her indifferently. His attitude
now effectively erased whatever lingering warmth she
held over from two nights ago.

"I have a little gift for Diane. I thought it might cheer
her up." Eva reached into her pocket and pulled out a
pink store bag, holding it up for Maxwell to see. With
reluctance Maxwell pushed himself away from the door
frame and held the door open for her. Gesturing in an
exaggerated courtly way, he indicated she should enter.

"Welcome to my parlor," he said.

"Said the spider to the fly," Eva finished, matching
his sarcastic tone. As he closed the door behind her, Eva
faced the room. It was beginning to show signs of slipping into another state of wreckage. She stood shaking
her head, without realizing it, in disbelief.

"Don't start getting ideas about cleaning," Maxwell
said directly behind her. The hairs on the back of Eva's

neck stood straight and electrified with his nearness. She turned half around to face him and immediately had to look up to his face.

"I only have to be told once where I'm not wanted," she answered blandly. "Clean it yourself. Better still, why not let Lavona do it?"

Eva was surprised at the dry laugh that shook Maxwell's shoulders once.

"What? Does Lavona look like the kind of woman to be a good housekeeper?" Maxwell asked with skepticism.

"You would know better than I," Eva said, moving a step away from him.

Adam raised his brows, opening his light eyes wide. "Lavona is good at one thing. I can tell you for a fact it isn't housekeeping." He turned away from Eva and walked with loose long-legged strides to knock softly at Diane's door.

"You have company," he said and moved back into the living room.

For the first time since entering the house, Eva noticed a long table set up for Adam to work at. There was a good desk light that had a long adjustable neck. Maxwell went over to it and eased his large frame onto a stool. Picking up a pair of tweezers, he continued with his dissection of what appeared to be some kind of sea plant with bulbous fronds for leaves. In genuine interest Eva walked over and stood opposite him to watch silently as his huge hands with ease and sure control delicately separated the nodes and pods from the stem. Maxwell's eyes flickered up at her once, briefly.

"Why don't you take off your raincoat. You're dripping water on my floor," he said caustically.

"Sorry...I didn't realize it would make a difference,"

Eva softly shot back. Maxwell grunted, but she saw a reluctant corner of his wide mouth quirk upward with amusement.

Eva had the slicker off and was pushing up the long sleeves of her sweater when Diane's door opened and the youngster emerged. She wore a pair of shorts just a bit too snug for her and a T-shirt. As she limped gingerly from the back room, her hands were busy putting her stubborn unruly hair in order.

"Is Dory here?" Diane asked, rounding the corner into the living room and finally spotting Eva. "Oh…it's you. I thought Dory was here," she said with barely disguised disappointment.

The thought that she'd be brightening the little girl's day was quickly squelched with Eva. She grinned ruefully to herself. It was only natural that Diane would want someone her own age to visit.

"Hello, Diane. How's it going?"

"Okay," Diane said distantly, shrugging. Eva frowned and turned to look questioningly at Maxwell, only to find that apparently he wasn't paying any attention to their exchange as he continued to bend over his work.

"And your foot…is it getting better?"

Diane only nodded, standing so that the injured left foot was balanced on top of the right. She finished twisting her hair into place and stood quietly looking down at the floor. It was not going exactly as Eva had planned, and now she felt foolish for even coming.

"Well…I only stopped by quickly to say hello." Eva looked behind her to the pink bag. "Oh! And I got you a little present." She passed it to Diane, who took it grudgingly, still not looking directly at Eva.

"Hey! You know better than that," Maxwell coaxed low behind them. Eva turned to find him sitting back on the stool, his hands braced stiffly on the edges, forcing the sinewed muscles of his arm and shoulders to press taut through his shirt.

"Thank you," came the whispered response from Diane.

Eva sighed, not understanding what had gone wrong. She picked up her slicker. "Well…I guess I'll be leaving. Maybe it will be sunny tomorrow and you can…"

"Why didn't you come?"

Eva faced Diane again. "Pardon me?" she asked, confused.

"Why didn't you come? The other day I waited all day for you to come and see me."

Eva stared openmouthed at Diane. "Why didn't I…but I did come by!"

Diane still looked doubtful. Eva turned a confused face to Maxwell who was listening closely now, his own brows drawn together in thought.

"Diane…" Eva started again carefully. "The morning after your accident, I did come by to see you. I was going to stay a little while and then take the ferry into St. Thomas, but Lavona said you were sleeping."

Diane frowned. "I was in my room, but I wasn't asleep. I was hoping that you'd stay with me instead of…" Diane's eyes shot contritely to her father and then dropped sullenly to her bare feet.

Once again Eva turned to Maxwell, as he let out a deep breath and stood up. Putting his hands flat in the back pockets of his jeans, he pursed his lips and walked slowly over to stand next to Eva. His expression was closed, and he stood for a long moment looking thoughtfully at his daughter. Adam's jaw tensed, and his eyes dropped to Eva and then back to Diane.

"I know that Diane likes you, Eva. I was going to ask

you if you didn't mind staying with her a few hours that day but…'' He looked fully at Eva again, talking directly to her, and for the first time since she'd known him, it was seriously and without derision or indifference. ''Lavona came by from the Hamiltons' and said she'd stay.'' Maxwell shrugged. ''There didn't seem to be any point in bothering you if she was here. You know what I'm saying?'' Maxwell questioned in his deep voice.

''Yes,'' Eva answered, wondering if she and Maxwell were now thinking the same thing, that Lavona may have deliberately kept Eva from Diane. For what reason was anyone's guess. ''I told her to tell you that I came by,'' Eva said to Diane, ''but I'm sure she just forgot.'' Eva defended Lavona weakly and without any enthusiasm.

''I'm sure,'' Maxwell said in a strange voice, still watching Eva closely.

Eva broke the look between them, not sure of what she was seeing in that penetrating gaze. ''Well, it doesn't matter. Why don't you open your present, Diane. See if you like it.''

When Diane extracted the two books and the hair barrettes, she finally broke into a smile and came over to stand shyly in front of Eva.

''Thank you, Eva.''

''You're welcome, dear. Here…let's put these in your hair and see how they look.'' Eva took them and clamped them into the thick hair. ''There! Why don't you go find a mirror and see what you think?''

''Okay!'' Diane beamed cheerfully and went off to her room.

Eva crossed her arms over her chest and stood awkwardly in the ensuing silence, very much aware of Maxwell right behind her. She stole a quick glance at him to find him watching her intently, that same searching, examining look he'd given her the first time she'd seen him on the ferry coming from St. Thomas. But this look was not superficial or impersonal. Diane came back.

"It looks good!" she proclaimed.

"I'm glad. Enjoy them." Eva smiled at the little girl. Her mind suddenly came up with another idea. Spontaneously she looked from Diane to her father. "Look…how would you like to come to my house for dinner? Nothing great, you understand, but…"

"Ooooh! Could we, Daddy?" Diane pleaded.

Maxwell nodded agreement, more quickly than Eva would have believed. It surprised her and she raised her brows in question.

"Fine with me," Adam said evenly, and he was drowned out by Diane's exuberant reaction. "Go put some clothes on," he admonished his daughter, and Diane was off like a shot. Then he went back to his worktable and began to wrap and jar his samples.

"I'm sorry to interrupt your work. Maybe we should do this another time," Eva said uncertainly.

"Are you really going to now tell Diane that you've changed your mind?" he asked, arching a brow at her.

Eva tilted her head at him pertly. "Diane can still come. You can stay here if you want to work."

Maxwell looked suggestively up and down her lithe form in the casual but well-fitting jeans. "Afraid to be alone with me again?" he asked her softly.

Eva raised her chin and gave him a slight, defiant smile. "If I was afraid of that, I'd only have invited Diane."

"But you still have to prove that you're not, don't you? Is that also why you came by so bright and early the other morning?"

Eva's eyes widened to stare silently at him. He was so

close to the truth that she couldn't think of a thing to respond with. She did want to prove that she wasn't going to make a mountain out of a molehill, but something deep within her had been touched and awakened, and it was frightening. It was frightening because the feelings had been stirred by Maxwell and she didn't want him to be able to do that to her. She certainly didn't want him to know that he could.

"It's only dinner we're talking about, Maxwell. Nothing more," Eva answered him in a tightly controlled voice. But he only sort of grinned wickedly at her and continued putting his things away.

Eva walked away wondering if she was really so transparent. A chill of apprehension caused her to shiver as she shrugged her way into her slicker and buttoned it. Behind her was this strange wall of heat. It reached out to flicker up and down her back seductively, tempting her closer and closer to its soothing warmth. But she wouldn't give in to it, knowing that Maxwell was the radiating source.

A STEEL BAND PLAYED music from the radio positioned on the curved counter just outside the kitchen. Diane knelt on the indoor-outdoor green carpeting in front of the coffee table, looking through an old magazine and nibbling on a nearby dish of pretzels. Maxwell was still setting the small square table as Eva began to bring out plates of food.

"Okay, it's ready," she said, maneuvering around Maxwell. She couldn't quite get used to this giant of a man carefully laying out napkins and water goblets. Maxwell always gave her the impression of being kind of chauvinistic and generally expecting all sorts of things to be done for him. Stranger still, Eva had not asked him to help set the table.

"Time to eat, Diane," he called to his daughter, and she got up at once and came to the table. They all sat down to eat.

Maxwell frowned and picked over his plate gingerly with his fork. "What is all this?" he asked cautiously. Eva shot him a withering look.

"You don't have to eat it," she said indifferently. "I can always make you a cheese sandwich or something else bland."

"I hate cheese sandwiches!" Diane grimaced, beginning to eat the food in front of her.

"I guess I can take it," Maxwell said conceding. But Eva smiled into her plate knowing, with total surprise, that Maxwell had been teasing her!

With the aid of the one lone cookbook in the kitchen on Caribbean cuisine, Eva had attempted to put together an authentic island meal. She'd thawed and baked several pieces of chicken in a casserole with okra and fungi. Eva had to admit that her fungi needed a little work. There was also salad and one other side dish.

They were almost through the meal when Diane pointed to the flat, sweet, delicately sauteed foodstuff.

"This is good. What is it?" the little girl asked.

Eva hesitated, feeling mischief bubbling within her. She looked at Diane and with a straight face said, "Fried bananas..."

Diane looked at her, and in the next instant they were both laughing over their private joke. Maxwell watched them both. He raised his brows not understanding what was so funny but didn't ask for an explanation. Eva realized that she and Diane were very likely making it funnier than it really was, but after three days of being cooped up inside, Diane was enjoying it.

When Eva began to clear the table, Diane wandered over to a small telescope on a tripod in a corner of the deck's far side and curiously tried to work it. Adam walked over and in a low voice began to explain the mechanics. As Eva scraped and washed dishes, she was happy to see Adam's patient attentiveness to his daughter. While Diane's accident had been more frightening than it was serious, it had apparently also served the purpose of awakening Maxwell to Diane's need for his attention. Maybe her needs weren't so far from his own, since Adam didn't seem to be the happiest person Eva had ever met.

Diane loved her father and needed his love. Perhaps Maxwell was admitting to the same kind of need himself. Eva had recognized that without the cynicism and indifference, Maxwell was a personable man. He was intelligent and while his sense of humor had so far shown itself to her as sardonic, she had a feeling it could be equally nonsensical and mischievous. He was good-looking, and there was no denying his strong masculine appeal—he was all man. But he needed a softer edge as far as Eva was concerned. However, she reasoned, Maxwell didn't take her seriously in any case, so her exercise in trying to know and understand him was useless.

Eva was deep in thought as she went through the mechanics of cleaning up. She jumped when she heard Maxwell's deep voice behind her.

"You really are domestic, aren't you?"

She glanced briefly over her shoulder at him and turned back to rinse the glass in her hand. "So...what's wrong with that?"

"Nothing. It's probably how you really are most of the time."

Eva laughed softly. "Maxwell, you don't know how I really am most of the time. You seem to enjoy making snap judgments based on little fact. You know something? I bet your wife was very independent and you resented it…"

Eva rinsed another glass, put it on the drain, and picking up a towel leaned back against the tiny sink and dried her hands. Maxwell was staring at her with a mixture of cold hard anger and something else, some other emotion she couldn't name. His mouth was a grim straight line, and his jaw tensed repeatedly. Eva was fascinated, again not sure what it was she'd said to achieve that look from him.

"Close…but no cigar," Maxwell answered cryptically. "I married one kind of woman and ended up with another kind." He left it at that.

"Then I guess I was luckier," Eva said evenly. "Kevin and I always understood each other perfectly. It was nice." Eva smiled softly, dreamily, not catching the painful expression on Maxwell's face, his mocking scowl disguising it. "I always loved Kevin…since I was about fourteen," Eva added ruefully, a little embarrassed at her admission of youthful devotion to one person. "I never thought of marrying anyone else." She looked up at the grunt and deep-chested chuckle from the man across from her.

"It sounds more like a habit than love."

Eva stared long at him. "I'm beginning to think you don't know what love is, Adam Maxwell. That's a real shame…for you," she ended softly.

Eva moved quickly past him and out onto the gallery. She took a deep breath of the cool night air, noting that the rain had stopped. Diane had made it to the sofa and was curled up in a childish ball fast asleep. Eva casually dropped the blue afghan from the back of the sofa over the sleeping form. Maxwell walked slowly over to stand and look down at his sleeping daughter. He carefully lifted her in his arms and carried her through the open French doors that led to Eva's bedroom. While he put Diane on the bed, Eva let out a sigh of contentment, but one mixed curiously with alertness and wariness.

They walked back into the other room and the gallery suddenly went dark as Maxwell turned out the light. Eva tried to see where he stood, but there was only a crescent moon that hadn't risen high enough yet to allow her to. She turned and walked the length of the gallery, all the way to the end. The evening, for the most part, had been lighthearted and easy. But with it almost over and Diane asleep, a now familiar, threatening fear began to descend over Eva like a veil.

She could feel Maxwell somewhere behind her, although he never made a sound on the carpeting. Eva stood silently near the railing to the gallery, looking out on the bay at night with the lights from anchored vessels like diamonds in the distance. Maxwell reached her, leaning against a support column.

Maxwell's hand came up to touch with warm fingers the back of her neck. Immediately Eva stiffened.

"Easy..." Maxwell coaxed in a low, husky voice. Slowly Eva relaxed under the gentle massaging fingers. The slightly callused tips of his hand made sensuous little circles, and Eva was surprised at the gentleness. She was beginning to feel a soothing heat melt her limbs into soft pliancy.

"The dinner was terrific," Adam said in that comfortable low voice. "You're a good cook. But then, I knew you would be." There was the mocking tone now.

"I suppose it fits the image you have of me," Eva whispered ruefully, somewhat used to his ways by now. Her mind and senses continued to follow the large hand as the fingers slipped just inside the boat neckline of the sweater and began the massage of her shoulders. Maxwell didn't answer her question.

"Diane really likes you, you know that?"

"I like her, too. She's a nice friendly little girl." Eva turned a little toward Maxwell, his hand remaining on her back. "But what you think of her is more important."

"I'm beginning to see that."

"I'm surprised you never noticed. It's written all over her face."

There was the barest pressure on the back of Eva's neck and shoulders as she found herself moving a step closer to Maxwell. And then another.

"Maybe I wasn't paying enough attention," he said in low self-derision. "I guess I thought Diane came to visit because the divorce settlement said so. It was damned nice of the courts to allow me once-a-year rights to my own daughter," he said, his voice gaining in anger. "She comes down once a year, and each year I feel as if I know her less and less...two weeks just doesn't make it."

Eva felt gratified by the honest expression of feelings Maxwell had for his child. And she felt absurdly pleased that he now chose to talk honestly to her about them.

"I know it's hard. But she's growing fast. You should talk to her, tell her as simply as you can how things are. She'll understand, Maxwell." Eva tried to see his eyes. "Your daughter loves you..."

Eva found herself even closer to him, and Maxwell's

other hand came up to her shoulders. She was now standing right in front of him. "I swear, you must be a lawyer. If not then you should be. You argue a very convincing case."

His head was starting to bend toward her. Eva could hear his deep-chested breathing; she stood in anticipation.

"I—I'm not arguing. And I only work in a law office…" Eva whispered. His lips were very near.

"I was close…"

"Common sense would have…Maxwell?"

"Shh."

Their lips touched gently. Adam's mouth rolled across Eva's lips, moistening the curves with his tongue. His hands were slow but firm, gathering her close to his chest and thighs. A tingling began in her toes.

Eva's hands rose and were sandwiched between them spread over his chest. Under the palms she could feel his heartbeat. Maxwell pressed harder, and Eva opened her mouth giving him access.

It was beginning again. Like the other night. Some other woman had taken over and she was willingly in his arms again. What had happened to her? Why was this so easy…and right? Eva liked kissing him, liked the feel and move of his mouth on hers. How long had it been since anyone had kissed her this way…? *Oh, Kevin! I'm sorry!* The kiss seemed endless. Her knees weakened. She leaned into him for added support.

Slowly Adam's hands were stroking her back. On the third trip down they came up under the loose hem of her sweater. Her skin at first shivered, then warmed to the touch. Maxwell's hands slid sensuously up the side of her torso, the thumbs riding her rib cage until finally he encountered the soft underside of her breasts.

Eva's reaction was slower in coming this time, Adam's

kiss much more studied and seductive. Their mouths separated and he kissed her cheek.

"Max…" she breathed against his throat. She didn't struggle at all, but Adam let some space separate their warm bodies and Eva adjusted her sweater.

"This sounds familiar…" Maxwell murmured.

"That's because it is." Eva's voice was a whisper and unsteady.

"Eva, I know you enjoyed it as much as I did," he added with a touch of impatience.

"That's beside the point." She pushed at his chest to create more space.

"Then what is the point?" he asked in a low growl.

Eva looked up at him, into his ruggedly handsome face. This could happen again. She had set a precedent for Adam holding and kissing her. But she knew that Maxwell was not a man to just let it stop with holding and kissing. She looked seriously into his face hoping that he could see her eyes and her confusion.

"I don't know you. I don't understand you all the time…" Her voice was still low.

"I'm not all that complicated," he responded, rubbing her shoulders.

"And I'm not even sure that I like you!" Eva also confessed.

"Just as long as you're not positive." Eva heard the amusement in his voice. It made her a little angry that he might not be taking her seriously in this instance. He put his arms around her waist and pulled her back to his chest. Eva's hands came to try and keep the space between them.

"No…stay here," he commanded in a deep voice. Eva relaxed the taut muscles in her arms. Finally when she became less stiff, he let out a deep sigh and lightly kissed her forehead. The gesture surprised her.

"Look…there isn't very much to know."

Eva frowned, lifting her shoulders helplessly. "It's—it's more than that."

"What more?"

She looked straight ahead to the opening of his shirt. With a forefinger she pressed through the opening to gently brush through the curly chest hair; it was so soft. She thought frantically how to put it into words. How do you tell a man that you're afraid of the way he makes you feel, because you've never felt that way before…not even with your husband. How do you tell him you think you find it exciting, but please not to go so fast…and not to hurt you. How does one tell a man like Adam Maxwell that you don't want to be treated like Lavona Morris, casually…and easily dismissed from thought, one day to the next.

Eva let out a shallow sigh. She was dismally aware right now of her inexperience. She had no clear idea how to deal with Adam in this situation.

"What more? I—I don't know…" she lied, hating the sudden coward in herself.

"What is it you want from me then?" he asked a little coldly.

Eva looked up at him again. "Respect. No judging. No ridicule. No indifference…that's all."

"Have I been so hard on you?" he questioned.

Had he been? Their eyes held for a long, breathless moment. Once more she turned a direct answer away. "I don't know what you want from me either, Maxwell."

Adam drew in a long breath and groaned in a decidedly suggestive manner. His large hands roamed over her shoulders and down her back. Again his hands took liberties, working their way under her sweater, sliding over the skin and making her hold her breath as he pulled her against him. "I don't think you want to know," he whispered.

Eva gasped. "You're impossible! You're the most conceited, arrogant person I've ever met!" she said with feeling.

He chuckled dryly. "I've been called worse." Adam grabbed her chin in his hand and lowered his head to kiss her once more, silencing the words and warming the coolness of her tone.

Eva realized that Adam Maxwell held a tremendous power over her, though she wasn't sure he knew it. As she went soft in his arm and ended a halfhearted struggle, she also knew she'd have to work overtime not to lose control with him completely. But without ever being fully conscious of it, she was kissing him back just as eagerly, responding naturally. And the other thought she did not allow herself was that if Adam ever pressed her further, she may not really want to stop him.

Adam drew back. Eva suddenly lamented her inability to see his face in the dark, to see his eyes. She wondered if he was at all as rattled as she was. "Ummm…your mouth is still very soft," he murmured, resting his hands on her waist, "and your kiss is getting better."

"Kevin never complained," Eva said dreamily, without thinking. Of course Kevin's kisses had not been so thoroughly consuming. Maxwell was very quiet for a time. Then he released her completely and leaned against the pillar, crossing his arms. Eva felt his distinct withdrawal away from her. Not only physically, but emotionally as well. She was puzzled.

"You must have had a good marriage to talk so easily about him now."

"We did," Eva softly confirmed, although she made no mention of the off-and-on guilt she felt in allowing another man to touch her so intimately.

"Well, I can't say the same," Maxwell whispered roughly. He pushed away from the pillar and moved around Eva to brace his hands on the low railing. She could just see the bunching of tensed muscles in his upper arms. He was all tight again.

"Max?" Eva called, the shortened name slipping out unnoticed. She barely touched a hand to his shoulder. "Do—do you want to talk about it?"

"No!" he responded, and Eva drew back at once. "You were right about one thing. You were luckier. My wife and I...well, it just didn't work."

"That's not altogether true," Eva whispered. "You have Diane between you. There must have been some feeling there."

Maxwell's head turned in her direction, and slowly he stood to his full height. His light eyes pierced the dark to see her, and Eva was sure they'd both communicated some basic thought and feeling to each other. He began moving toward her, and Eva's heart began to pound, wondering what he had in mind as he reached out for her.

There was a rustling in the dark and then Diane's sleepy voice, "Daddy?"

The magic spell starting to take hold of Maxwell and Eva was gone.

"Daddy," Diane called again.

"I'm right here, Diane," Maxwell said, but still looking at Eva. It was she who turned away first, and slowly walked over to where Diane was untwisting herself from the crocheted afghan.

"Well...good morning!" Eva teased, smiling as the little girl stood in the bedroom doorway rubbing her eyes.

"It's not morning," Diane said with just a touch of uncertainty in her voice.

"No, it's not," her father agreed, coming forward to face her. "But it will be if we don't get home."

"Ahhhhh! Do we have to? We just got here...I was having a good time!" Diane fussed.

Eva laughed at that.

"How would you know? You fell asleep!" Maxwell said caustically.

"I'm glad you had a good time," Eva inserted, "but I think your father is right."

Diane pouted.

"Diane..." her father said in warning. Diane thought for a fast second, seeing the hard set to her father's face.

"Okay," she said, making the right decision.

"Maybe you'll come again," Eva suggested, but knew in her heart it was more for Maxwell's sake than Diane's that she said so. As if sensing the flow of her thoughts, Maxwell looked pointedly at her.

"Maybe," he said, his expression unreadable.

"Goodnight, Eva," Diane said, and surprised everyone when she came over to Eva and reached to kiss her cheek. "Thank you for dinner. It was good...even the bananas!"

Eva smiled at her. "I'm glad you enjoyed it. Goodnight, dear."

Diane began heading down the stairs to the waiting Jeep. Maxwell faced Eva and put his hands in his pants pockets. Eva just looked at him, waiting for him to speak. She was suddenly remembering the first time they'd stood together on the gallery discussing Diane and had ended up in each other's arms kissing with abandon. Eva blinked rapidly and looked down at her sandaled feet.

"You know Carnival starts next week," Maxwell said.

"I know. It sounds as if it's going to be quite an event," Eva commented.

"The people here love a chance to play music and get together to share food." Eva nodded. Maxwell continued. "You might enjoy it. There's music playing Thursday night down in Cruz Bay…"

Eva took a deep breath and stopped him. "I—I know. I'm planning on going."

Maxwell frowned. "Alone?"

Again she looked down at the green carpeting. "No…I'm going with someone."

"I didn't know you knew people here," Maxwell said skeptically.

"Well…I don't, really," Eva said a little weakly.

"Then whom are you going with?" Although his deep voice held genuine curiosity, there was also an underlying tone that sent a chill through Eva. It was almost censuring.

"I met someone on St. Thomas several days ago."

Maxwell did stiffen and straighten now. But Eva was starting to feel put upon and indignant. Who was he anyway to question what she did?

"You mean you picked up someone?" he said sarcastically, and it somehow washed away all the comfortable atmosphere that had existed between them all evening.

"I don't do things like that," Eva said stiffly with a frown.

"Oh? Then he picked you up?"

Eva knew Adam was doing this deliberately. She let out a controlling breath. She wasn't going to let Adam manipulate her.

"He's a local cabdriver. He was very nice and helped me with my luggage when I first came and wasn't sure where to go. And the other day on St. Thomas when I lost…"

"You don't have to explain to me," Adam said indifferently, half turning away.

Eva watched him with amazement. "You're right! You don't rate an explanation!" Eva stood straight and crossing her arms over her small chest, glared at him. "Goodnight, Maxwell!"

Adam tensed his jaw, letting his mouth tighten. He quirked a brow, letting his eyes sweep over her rather insolently. He never said another word as he turned and caught up to his daughter waiting below.

Eva, who had never been given to cursing, tightly clenched her teeth and muttered "Bastard!" with a good deal of satisfaction under her breath. And then she almost immediately felt let down. She would have liked, above all things, to have gone to the festivities with Maxwell.

Chapter Six

Eva's anger was just enough to last one full day, and it kept her away from Hawksnest and the possibility of seeing Adam Maxwell. By the end of the second day, it had burned itself out, but she remained home nonetheless.

Milly Decker stopped by to see how she was doing in the hillside house and stayed most of the afternoon to visit. That evening Eva drove into Cruz Bay for a lone dinner at one of the small, open-air, unpretentious restaurants and stayed to watch the feature film, which began at eight o'clock. It was about a hijacked New York City subway train. Eva thought the story, at worst, absurd, but it was entertaining and kept her from thinking of other things.

Twice during the evening local men made attempts to gain her attention, but she was unresponsive and aloof, remembering how Maxwell had accused her of picking up Deacon Butler in St. Thomas. It annoyed her to some degree that she would restrict her responses based on what Maxwell thought, even though she doubted that the men were just merely being friendly. She certainly was not of a mind to be anything more. So she ignored them.

When the movie was over, Eva followed the small crowd of people out of the restaurant. Some walked to nearby residences, while others headed for their cars or taxi services. It was as the crowd was thinning that she noticed Adam Maxwell. Eva immediately looked to see if Lavona was with him but could only pick out the small child frame of Diane walking next to her father.

Eva had not seen them enter the restaurant and wasn't really sure they'd even seen the movie, but she wasn't prepared to face Maxwell yet. Eva slowed her steps to a stroll and moved in the shadows of the palm trees until Adam and Diane had climbed into their Jeep and headed out of town.

The next day she played her radio very low and sat curled on the sofa of the gallery reading. A number of times there was a car on the road below her. She'd stiffen momentarily, half expecting one of the cars to be Adam's. But it never was. So the following day when she was prepared for more of the same solitude, she was truly surprised when a car did stop below and there was the sound of footsteps climbing toward her.

Eva was seated at the circular counter space drinking iced tea and writing a letter when Maxwell reached the gallery. She turned her head at his approach and then was on her feet in total wonder. Maxwell stood before her in a pair of white drawstring pants of a lightweight cotton and a royal-blue tank shirt with white piping around the sleeves and neck. The whole length of his muscular arms was exposed, as well as a band of his stomach, visible below the hem of his shirt. They stood for a moment silently watching each other, Eva now self-conscious in the black halter swimsuit she wore under a pair of very brief white shorts. Her round feminine curves were shown off to their best advantage in the black suit, and the brevity of the shorts made her legs seem longer than they were. She'd not bothered curling her hair since her first few days on the island, and the short haircut was now layered straight and flat, pixie fashion, down her forehead and the sides of her face.

"Hello," Eva opened with a false lightness, as her heart thudded once against her chest. Maxwell did not respond with a greeting.

"You sound as if you're surprised to see me," he commented, tilting his head a little to the side and looking her up and down rather slowly. Eva crossed her arms in what she hoped was a casual movement.

"I am."

"I told Diane you were probably busy since we haven't seen you." He came forward to lean against the counter with his hip, also crossing his arms over his chest. She realized he now had the advantage since she had to tilt her head in order to see into his face. It was also not lost on Eva that apparently only Diane had missed her presence the last several days.

"I was," she answered, trying to seem indifferent.

Maxwell's lightly browned eyes looked into hers, searching over her features. "Doing what?" he asked softly.

"Laundry," she improvised quickly, "visiting with Mildred Decker..." Which was the truth.

Maxwell held her gaze for a second longer. Then his eyes dropped to the half-finished letter on the counter next to him. He looked up at her, quirking a questioning brow. Defensively Eva put the letter face down under a nearby fruit bowl. "Letter to someone you left behind?" he asked mockingly.

Eva raised her chin. "Yes, as a matter of fact. My mother!" She moved then to put some space between them. "Why are you here?"

Maxwell stood straight and put his hands into the

pockets of the light pants. The fabric gave way under the force of his large hands and the pants slid from his waist to his hips, showing even more of his stomach lightly covered with hair. Eva's imagination suddenly went wild, wondering if he had on swim trunks or anything under the pants. She lowered her eyes to her bare feet.

"I'm going over to Coral Bay. It's the other side of the island. Diane thought you'd like to go. Have you been there yet?"

"No." She shook her head.

"Okay...then why don't..."

"Maxwell..." Eva interrupted "...considering how we last parted company maybe...well, maybe I shouldn't go."

He seemed to think about that for a moment, frowning. "How did we part company?" he asked blandly. Eva was infuriated by his calm and apparent dismissal of the evening. Did he take nothing seriously?

"I'd say angrily," Eva answered stiffly.

"I wasn't angry," Maxwell said, turning away from her.

"Well, I was!" Eva almost exploded in exasperation.

Maxwell had one foot on a descending step. "I know. Are you coming?" he finished.

Eva stared openmouthed at him. She was right. He had just brushed the whole episode aside. She finally let out a sigh of resignation. "Yes, I'll come."

"I'll wait in the Jeep," he said and disappeared. Eva stared silently at the space he'd just occupied, wondering if she would ever understand him.

Eva went to retrieve a white cotton sweater. She got her tote and filled it with things she thought she'd need if she was gone all day. All the time she wondered about the mercurial changes in Maxwell's moods. They hadn't seen or spoken to each other in almost four days, and then he just shows up as though nothing had happened. That she had thought about him for those four days, imagined him in the arms of Lavona Morris, didn't for the moment enter into her thinking as she went to meet him.

Eva climbed into the front passenger seat and immediately he started the engine. She looked around her. ''Where's Diane? Did you leave her at the house?''

Maxwell backed up and turned the Jeep around, shifting gears quickly. ''Diane's not going with us.''

Eva frowned in confusion. ''But you said she suggested...''

''That's right. But I never said she would be coming with us.''

Eva looked at him, trying to figure out what this meant. He cast a quick look in her direction and back to the road.

''Want to change your mind? I'll take you back...''

''No! No...it's okay.''

Maxwell nodded and continued driving. Still confused and also surprised now, Eva settled into her seat for the journey. Somewhere in her mind she worked out that Maxwell was not the kind of man to have anyone for company just for the hell of it. She reasoned finally that she was here because he wanted her to be. Her spirits began to lift.

''Where is Diane?'' she asked.

''With Dory Hamilton. Dory and two of her brothers are in the parade next weekend for Carnival. There's still work to do on their costumes. Diane's going to be with them until Wednesday.''

''I'm surprised she didn't want to come with you,'' Eva commented.

Adam shrugged. "I'm glad she's made friends here. It's no fun being with me all the time."

"Diane used to think so. What happened?" she asked with some concern.

"I don't know for sure. Maybe she realizes that I'm always going to be here for her. She doesn't have to worry about losing me."

"So it makes it easier for her to find other friends," Eva concluded.

"Yeah, I guess so. Anyway, she says she's having a great summer," Maxwell said.

"I'm very glad to hear that." Eva relaxed. "But then…why did she tell you to ask me along?"

Maxwell turned his head to regard her, his eyes squinting, his jaw looking very square and strong, jutting into the breeze. "She said, so I wouldn't be lonely," he said evenly. "She said you'd make a good assistant in her place."

"What about Lavona?" Eva couldn't help asking in a low voice. Adam looked away a bit impatiently and took his time answering.

"She had other plans," was all he said.

They followed the Center Line Road through the National Parklands of St. John, passing scenic views and old ruins. Coral Bay was a very small town on the other side of St. John with a beautiful harbor lined with a number of small sailing crafts. Maxwell parked the Jeep near the pier and they walked from there. If Cruz Bay was a tiny town, Coral Bay was tinier still, with only a handful of shops and restaurants. Eva walked beside the towering form of Maxwell, feeling oddly complacent and safe with him. People called out to him, waving, and it surprised her that so reticent a man would have friends here.

They finally came to a stop outside a green-painted

cement hut. Maxwell knocked on the door, and after a
bit of muffled movement the door opened to show an
elderly black man, his tightly curled hair all white, his
teeth clamped on a very worn pipe.

"Hey, man. You make it after all!" he said in his
musical tongue, opening the door for them to enter. Maxwell had to duck into the very low door frame. Once
inside he could stand straight again, but Eva was sure
there weren't two inches to spare between the ceiling and
the top of Adam's head.

"This is Lito Varrick," Adam said to Eva. "Lito, this
is Eva Duncan. She's vacationing here from New Jersey."

Lito nodded politely, his white teeth even and brilliant
in his shiny dark face. "Yes, yes! It's good to see you,
man. How you like St. John?" he asked Eva.

She was always amused at the local use of the word
"man" to describe just about anyone and anything. She
smiled at the gentleman. "Oh, I love it here! It's a beautiful, peaceful island."

"That's good!" Lito beamed at her. "Many continen-
tals they say it too hot, man. Nothing to do."

Eva's smile widened, aware that Adam was watching
and listening to the exchange between her and Lito. "I've
only been here for a short time. But I feel as if I've lived
here for years!"

Lito laughed. "That's good. Adam find woman who
like it here, too."

Eva raised her brows in an ironic gesture at Maxwell
and then back to Lito. "Well, he didn't exactly find me,"
Eva inserted caustically. That sounded too much like he'd
just picked her up somewhere, and she was still somewhat sensitive to that kind of reference. For another thing
Lito made it sound as though it was all Adam's doing,

and she'd had no part in deciding whether or not to be with him.

Eva looked again at Adam, but his attention was now focused on a large tank on a table, filled with plants and shells. He had his hand in the tank almost up to his elbow, poking through the growth. Eva grimaced ruefully and turned back to Lito. "That's what's really important to him..." she whispered, nodding toward the tank.

Lito laughed softly around his pipe stem. "Maybe. But I not so sure," he said mysteriously.

"Lito, what do you have for me today?" Maxwell's voice broke into their quiet conversation, and Lito walked over to stand next to Maxwell and talk. The conversation was obviously on fish and sea plants, so Eva left them alone, not wanting to interfere, and not able to contribute.

She found a comfortable low chair covered in a bright flowered pattern and sat in it. Eva looked around the room. It was very neat and clean but lacked most definitely any female touches. Lito Varrick was either a bachelor or a widower.

After turning her head around the room, Eva noticed a sleeping gray cat across the back of her chair. The cat lazily opened one eye halfway, gave her a disinterested look, and went peacefully back to sleep. She smiled at the action and turned back to the two men, listening to their low voices.

The conversation was technical, all about fungus and water temperatures, phosphate levels and oxygen contents. She'd always been impressed with Maxwell's knowledge of such things, and it was clear to her now that he had also made the best use of his time by becoming acquainted with someone who lived here, knew the waters and the islands, and could teach him more. Eva watched the concentration on Maxwell's face, the wide mouth pursing or forming questions, the jaw tensing thoughtfully, the hands gentle with the fragile sea life. What a study in contrasts he was.

The gray cat behind her padded silently down the arm of the chair and onto Eva's lap, taking the liberty of curling up into a furry ball and going back to sleep. Eva idly stroked the soft thick fur, thinking more about the enigma that was Adam Maxwell.

Half an hour later, the two men turned away from the tank, drying their hands on towels.

"Well, that helps." Adam sighed. "Now I see what I did wrong."

"Not too bad, man. Next time remember to place your samples in salt water, not fresh."

"Okay, Lito." Adam nodded. Eva had never seen him defer to anyone else before. He respected and liked this older gentleman.

They both now turned to see her with the cat.

"Ahhh…Pepper likes you! That good. Pepper scratch Miss Lavona on leg last time, eh, Adam?"

Adam was watching Eva and lifted a brow at Lito's observation, but he made no comment and held no apology to Eva for having brought Lavona here also. Eva didn't expect any from him. They said good-bye to Lito and left the small hut.

Adam suggested lunch, and they stopped at the Sputnik. Over their lunch of fried fish and salad, Adam explained that Lito was a retired fisherman who was often called on by the Park Service for his expert advice on the sea world. He was always available to help Adam when he ran into a problem with his research. After lunch Adam continued to conduct Eva on a Jeep tour around the island.

She liked being with him like this, when he was informative and easy. Not closed in and careful. They stopped at Chocolate Hole, a different side of the island that was rocky coastline and no sandy beaches, where the water crashed to shore and where the sun rose on a flat low horizon. On the drive back they circled past the Annenberg ruins, an old sugar mill, but Adam said that tour was for another day since the sun was already going down.

Back at her house, Eva invited Adam to have dinner with her. He hesitated, but then shook his head no. "Not tonight. I have things to do."

"Oh," was Eva's response, not realizing yet her disappointment. "Thank you for letting me come today. I enjoyed it very much."

"Good. I'll pick you up tomorrow morning…"

"Tomorrow morning?" Eva questioned. He'd said nothing all day about taking her with him again.

"I thought you were going to be my assistant in place of Diane?" he said, frowning.

Eva shrugged. "I—I thought you were only kidding. I don't know how I can help."

"I'll show you how," he said smoothly, once again starting his engine to leave.

Eva gestured helplessly. "Well, okay. If you're sure…"

"I'll pick you up at seven." He waited.

"Fine. I'll be ready," Eva said a bit breathlessly. Already she was looking forward to it.

When Maxwell picked her up promptly the next morning, he was wearing the same loose-fitting pants and another tank shirt, this one a deep green. Eva chose to wear the same black swimsuit, worn under a one-piece short denim jump suit. There was almost no talk between them as Maxwell got them to the sailing vessel and quickly under sail. Occasionally he'd yell an instruction to her, and she'd follow it even though she was afraid she'd pull the wrong line or get something twisted.

The breeze was good and steady, and the vessel didn't lurch nearly as much as it had the week before. The ship held its course, and Maxwell was able to lock the tiller into one position, freeing him to move around the small ship. He stripped off his shirt and light drawstring pants and stood before Eva in his brown swim trunks. The color was not that much darker than his own skin color, and for a weird moment with the sun behind him he seemed naked. Eva drew in a sharp breath at the image which for a quick second proved extremely provocative and enticing. She knew an instant warming flow throughout her body.

Adam came and sat next to Eva taking hold of lines, lowering one sail, and raising another until the ship seemed to be sailing itself. He turned his head to find Eva staring at him with her almond-shaped eyes.

"You okay?" he asked, squinting against the bright sun.

Eva nodded, but she wasn't okay at all. Something was happening inside her that was different from any other time she'd been with Maxwell. It went beyond a lot of earlier feelings and reactions to him. She was beginning to feel intimidated, threatened, unsure all over again in his presence. She was sensing again his overwhelming maleness and virility, and part of her was struggling in its natural response to him.

"Who taught you to sail?" she asked in a queer, broken voice, diverting her thoughts to something safer.

Adam tied off another line. "I started learning in high school...picked it up again while in college. Troy Hamilton and Lito Varrick taught me the rest. They showed me how to handle the small-masted ships like a cutter or sloop when I first came down here.''

''How long have you been down here?''

''A little over three years.'' He braced a muscular leg against the side of the ship as he shifted a sail and the ship rolled. Eva tried to smooth down her wind blown hair with her hand.

''But why down here? Whom do you work for?''

Adam didn't answer right away, but then he turned to give her a quick, brief look of impatience. ''What is this...Twenty Questions?''

But Eva continued to wait for an answer. When he did choose to answer, it was almost with indifference.

''I'm with the research department of the National Oceanographic office in Washington...on loan from the Naval Department.''

Eva raised her brows appreciatively, and Maxwell gave a short chuckle. ''It's not as impressive as it sounds. You see what I do. It's not glamorous at all.''

''But it's fascinating. And looks like fun. And it's probably important work,'' Eva reasoned. Maxwell gave her a long thoughtful look.

''It is.''

The ship rolled in the opposite direction. Maxwell changed his seat, moving opposite Eva, and bracing his leg in reverse. Salt spray washed coolly over the side and splashed them lightly. Eva tilted her head and looked again at Maxwell. ''What are you in the Navy? An ensign?'' she asked, naming the only naval title she could remember.

Maxwell found the question amusing and laughed briefly, his teeth making a white slash in his brown face. ''Not even that. I don't have a position with the Navy. I'm a civilian employee.''

"I guess you must like it down here. It's been a long time."

Maxwell's grin slowly faded and his expression became guarded. "It's all right. No one bothers me down here."

"Are you hiding from someone?" Eva quipped teasingly, but the tensing of Maxwell's jaw suddenly alerted her to the lack of humor he found in her question.

"I can get another assignment anytime I want to. Right now, I don't want to. Being here suits me."

Eva hesitated a moment. "Maxwell, if you had an assignment stateside, you could see Diane more often," she pointed out. There was a long silence while he looked out to sea.

"I know," he answered her shortly. No doubt he'd already thought of his trade-off for being down here. But Eva didn't believe that the decision he'd made and held to was necessarily the right one…or an easy one for him.

"What about the rest of your family? Do you have any?" Eva could see the impatience with which he continued to view her questions, but still he answered her.

"My father lives in Boston. He's retired and spends all his time fishing. My mother died when I was eighteen. I have an older brother who lives in Colorado Springs with his wife and two sons. He teaches math at the Air Force Academy. End of questions…end of answers," he finished pointedly.

"It sounds as if you came from a military family. Were you a Navy brat?"

Maxwell sighed at her persistence. "No. Just a brat," he said caustically. Eva smiled at the comment, believing it.

Adam began dropping some of the sails after a few hours, and they were just off the cove of a small key.

Eva remained on board as Adam spent an hour in the water with the launch to catch small silvery pencil fish, sometimes diving to gather sea life from the sandy bottom.

She was coming to understand that Adam was not one for a lot of talk. The long silences with him were less awkward, and she did not take them or his glaring looks so personally. And there was also the undisputable knowledge that she wouldn't be here if he didn't want her to be. She was beginning to anticipate his moods and actions and sometimes even what he would say. Knowing all of this made it more fun to be with him.

And, too, Maxwell was not one to play games and waste time. He was very direct and straightforward but also much more sensitive than Eva had first given him credit for. It helped her in knowing and understanding him, even as she recognized that Maxwell would not give a damn what anyone thought of him.

When he finally surfaced for the last time, Eva was bending over the side with a widemouthed bucket attached to a line, ready to lower it to him. He put in his last catch and, as Eva pulled the bucket up, made his way to the launch and climbed in. Eva transferred his samples gingerly into the proper water-filled containers Adam had left for her. She expected him to come back on board, but when he didn't appear, Eva went back to lean over the side. Maxwell was standing up in the slightly bobbing dinghy, hands on his hips.

"Come on down, we're going to shore…and take off your jump suit. We're swimming in."

It was on Eva's lips to protest, but she said nothing. Apprehensively she did as she was told, climbing down the ladder into the launch. Maxwell's hands reached up to circle her waist and lift her the rest of the way. Goose bumps raised on her arms at the contact of his still damp hands.

"Maxwell…" she began, frowning at him, "I don't think I can do this. I can't swim!"

"Yes you can," he said positively in his firm deep voice. But he did see the concern on her face and reflected in the wide, appealing depths of her eyes. He squatted down next to her. "Look. We'll snorkel in. Remember all you have to do is breathe through the air hose and kick your feet. I'll hold on to you."

Eva took a deep breath and nodded. With shaking hands she put on her equipment and climbed over the side with Maxwell into the suddenly cold water. He held her tightly around the waist checking her mask and hose. Then he took her hand and pulled her gently away from the security of the boat. Together they headed toward the shore. Eva clutched convulsively to Maxwell's large hand, and every now and then he'd squeeze hers in reassurance. Her heart pounded in her chest, but slowly she began to relax, realizing that she was not going to sink even though the depth of the water had to be fifteen feet.

They were almost into shore when something rasped over the skin of Eva's neck and shoulder, causing a sudden burning sensation. Some sound came through her mouthpiece as she reached with her free hand to the tender spot. Maxwell, seeing that something was wrong, began kicking harder until he could stand in shallow water with her.

"What's the matter?" he asked, pulling off his mask.

Eva gasped for air, pulling off her mask and hose as well. "I—I don't know. Something scratched me… here," she said, rubbing her neck. Maxwell pulled her hand away.

"No...don't rub it. Come on. Let's get out of the water."

Once on the sandy beach Adam examined the injured area. His fingers probed gently and slowly, untying the straps of her suit to better reach the skin. Eva held her hand to her chest to keep the loosened suit in place.

"Looks like a jellyfish sting," Adam murmured, running his fingertips over the slowly rising welt on Eva's skin. "You okay?" he asked her softly.

Eva nodded, trying to hold the suit up and brush her hair from her face at the same time. Adam moved to stand tall in front of her. He took his own hands to brush her wet hair back.

"You sure?" he persisted.

"Yes, I'm fine." Eva smiled. She looked up at him so close to her and went still with the look of concern that quickly crossed his face.

"Maybe this wasn't such a good idea," he said in exasperation. Eva recognized that it was not directed at her.

"Maxwell, I'm fine," she said firmly. "It doesn't even sting so much now."

Nonetheless, he continued to search her face, and when he was finally assured that she told the truth, he patted her cheek. "All right...let's sit for a while."

They moved with their equipment up from the shore into the shadow of nearby low-lying palms.

"Leave that untied..." Maxwell pointed to her when she would have adjusted her suit. "It'll irritate the sting."

Eva nodded, holding the suit tightly to her chest, aware now in some embarrassment that her nipples were erect against the latex fabric. She sat on fallen dried leaves, bringing her knees up to her chest and hugging them to her so that her knees held the suit against her body. Maxwell stretched out beside her, leaning back until his powerful torso was supported on his elbows.

"You did okay out there," he said, without looking at her.

"Not bad for someone who can't swim," Eva joked nervously. "I must have been crazy to let you talk me into that!" But there was a smile in her voice.

"Were you scared?" Adam asked.

"A little at first. But as long as you held my hand I was fine," Eva readily admitted. Maxwell looked over his hunched shoulder at her.

"And except for the jellyfish," he added.

"How come you didn't get stung?" she asked indignantly.

Adam rolled onto his stomach, still supporting his body on his elbows. "A jellyfish with good taste.... What can I tell you."

"Baloney!" Eva said caustically. Adam looked up at her, his eyes dark and unreadable. They dropped to her raised thighs, to the exposed undersides.

"Jellyfish aren't the only ones you know..."

Eva frowned, not understanding his meaning.

"There's also gecko..."

"What's a gecko?" Eva asked suspiciously.

"A lizard," he answered casually. "It's about that long"—he held up the thumb and index finger of one hand to indicate three inches—"and it's brown and green, just like the one crawling up your side..."

Eva's eyes popped open and she gasped, pushing her legs straight out and looking down. Sure enough, a small creature slithered across her stomach and hopped onto the sand fleeing into the bushes.

"Maxwell!" Eva shouted in alarm, but Adam was

chuckling softly in his bass voice. "It's not funny!" Eva said, kicking sand at him.

Adam grabbed her ankle and pulled suddenly, bringing her off her bottom and flat on her back. Eva started to struggle in earnest, but she sputtered, went momentarily still, and pulling her leg out of Adam's grasp, she began to laugh.

Adam grabbed her other foot. "I thought you said it wasn't funny?"

"Maxwell...don't! That tickles!"

Adam looked down at her feet and back to her face. "Are you ticklish?" he asked in mock surprise.

"Yes!" Eva got out. Then she looked at him. "I mean, no!"

He began to crawl toward her.

"Maxwell, if you so much as touch me..."

"What? What will you do?" he asked as one of his hands moved and tickled along her arm. Then it moved to her throat.

"Maxwell..." Eva pleaded, but she was already laughing helplessly, trying to ward off his hands, which seemed to be so fast and suddenly everywhere. In self-defense Eva grabbed a handful of sand to throw at him. Seeing what she had in mind, Adam quickly captured her wrists and was half across her body holding the dangerous sand-clutched hand straight out.

Suddenly Eva stopped laughing and gasped again, looking down at her struggling body. The loosened swimsuit had been worked downward until her small high breasts were almost exposed. Maxwell looked, too. His clear brown eyes raised to hers, and Eva recognized at once a light in them she'd seen twice before. Eva was breathing hard from their tussle, and her chest rose and fell in agitation.

Adam let go of her wrist and slowly brought the hand to her heaving chest. Eva grabbed hold of his wide wrist with her own small hand with the intention of stopping him. But Adam was already moving the suit slowly lower until her breasts with their erect brown centers were completely visible.

Her other arm was under him and Eva couldn't move. But in that moment she never really thought to. This was the other thing happening inside her for days, the strange uneasiness that she was reluctant to put a name to. With it here again, about to happen, she knew it as a desire for Maxwell to touch and hold her again.

His fingers brushed across the tautly raised buttons of her breasts, and the touch sent a curling tension through her, warming and melting her.

"Maxwell..." Eva whispered, watching the muscles in his jaw, neck, and shoulders. Unbelievably, Maxwell lowered his mouth to completely cover one jutting breast in a moist, warm caress. His tongue moved erotically over the tip. Eva's eyes closed and she sighed deeply from within. Her hands closed into fists with the excruciating pleasure his touch suddenly brought. Her chest rose and fell, now in rising excitement.

Maxwell raised his head to look into her brown face to see her parted lips and closed eyes. He shifted positions to lie almost completely on her. His hands reached to cradle her head while he bent to kiss her waiting mouth. Eva answered his kiss with her own, letting him plunder delightfully the recesses of her mouth. Her arms came up around his neck to hold him to her. Adam let out a low groan and kissed her even deeper, more completely, like a hungry man.

She felt desire building within her until she thought she would faint. Adam was heavy across her body, and she could feel sand granules pressing into the skin of her shoulders, back, and legs.

Adam lifted his head to nibble playfully at her lips, to let his breath mix with the warmth of her own before once more settling on her mouth with his own little moan of pleasure. A fiery passion and a growing flame of need licked up and down Eva's spine, and for long delirious moments she was unaware of anything else.

He moved his mouth to her cheek, dragged it to her ear, down to her neck. Between them, his hands forced the black suit down further, and Eva did not resist. Briefly, boldly before she realized, Adam caressed her intimately and moved again up her stomach to her breasts. He slid his body down so that his mouth again could cover a breast, and Eva sensed it was too late to stop him. She wasn't sure she wanted to, but suddenly she was very scared. She began to tremble as his mouth explored her skin.

The trembling grew steadily, even as she was beside herself with a need she hadn't known for a very long time. Her hands clutched convulsively at Adam's shoulders. He was kissing her again, probing deeply with his tongue and pressing hard against her stomach. He released her mouth to kiss her throat and neck.

''Don't say no,'' he growled against her hot skin as if anticipating resistance. ''We're not kids. We know what this is about.''

''I—I know,'' she murmured breathlessly. But the shaking continued. Her worst insecurities surfaced, and she began to close down her feelings.

''We're both experienced...''

''No!'' Eva shook her head.

Adam suddenly stopped his movements. ''What?'' he asked raising his head.

"I mean...I'm not experienced. I—I haven't...oh, Max! I haven't been with anyone since Kevin. This—this is my first time since my husband. You're the first." Eva closed her eyes, turning her head so as not to see his disappointment.

Adam did look into her face a very long time, his eyes sweeping over her features. Slowly he lay to cover her, the only thing separating their pulsating bodies was Adam's swim trunks. His hand cupped her face.

"Do you want me to make love to you?" he asked hoarsely.

Eva nodded, her eyes still closed. There was a pause.

"Are you afraid?" Adam asked her. She nodded again. He let out a strained sigh and gave her a light reassuring kiss. "Don't be....I won't do anything you don't want me to."

Eva began to relax. She knew that Maxwell was not generally given to bending. That he would be so understanding now made her feel as though she'd turned an important corner in their chaotic relationship. Now she felt she could trust him, and she warmed toward him as she never had before. It went beyond the physical warmth of their mutual attraction for each other, and therefore it was much more intimate and personal.

Adam stood, bringing her naked form with him. He handed her the black suit. "I'm going to swim out and get the launch. You wait here."

And he turned away as she dressed, but then he tied the halter straps himself. It reminded Eva of her first day sailing with him when he helped her in and out of the life jacket.

It was midafternoon when they got under sail again. The wind was down and erratic, and Adam stayed at the tiller during the entire trip back. Eva felt awkward and didn't know what to say to ease the silence between them. Was he thinking of her as unsophisticated and slow? But he said nothing to indicate what his feelings were. He was the same unreadable Maxwell again.

Eva put on her jump suit against the sea breeze and sat alone away from him struggling with depression. Finally they were back in Hawksnest, but instead of taking her home as she thought he would, they headed for the Annenberg ruins. It was almost as if he were indicating that they couldn't separate for the rest of the day without some other action to change the mood.

The Annenberg was an old sugar mill, somewhat restored and now operated by the National Park Service. Tours were conducted there and along seashore walks to identify plant and sea life indigenous and transplanted to the area. On occasion natives of the island would demonstrate their age-old technique for basket weaving, or someone else would talk about how things used to be done on the island when they had only themselves and nature to rely on. But that afternoon the ruins were deserted.

Eva was glad because it meant she would not have to pretend an interest while her attention was really elsewhere. On the other hand, it placed her and Maxwell alone again.

In his usual knowledgeable way Adam told her the history of the sugar mill and the ongoing fight to preserve the remains. He talked by rote, and Eva had the impression that he spoke for want of anything else to do.

She was looking through a low arched stone window to another section of the ruin, conscious of Maxwell right behind her, talking in a low methodic tone. She wondered how he could be so calm and in control while she felt so tense inside. He stood with one hand in the pocket of the

drawstring pants and the other arm braced on the wall
over her head.

"These ruins are part of the history here, very much a
part of how things were done not so long ago…the burning of sugarcane and the extracting of the juices used in
producing rum…"

Eva moved away from the deep vibration of his voice
so close to her ear. She stood in a narrow doorway looking at the odd ovenlike openings on the walls.

"You can still see the carbon burned off on the stone
walls. There are dozens of ruins like this one all over the
island…" He was right behind her again. His breath
stirred the hair at her temple. If she turned around now,
he'd be right there, ready to…

Eva moved to a low wall, most of the stone brick
eroded away. She looked over the edge out to the beautiful sea with its fantasy colors, dotted with small islands
in the distance. Her back was warm. Adam was very
close to her, his broad chest wall behind her. He braced
his hands on the wall on either side of her. She was, in
essence, trapped.

"Eva…" his deep voice mumbled. She felt his mouth
at her neck, moving feather-light up to her ear, bringing
with the movement a tingling sensation down her spine.
Her heart thudded, and she brought her hands up to her
chest trying to stop the racing. Adam took her suddenly
by the waist and spun her into his arms, kissing her with
an urgency that startled her.

Her hands were trapped between them and she spread
them open on his green shirt feeling the padding of chest
hair underneath, feeling the powerful working of his
heart. Then her hands slipped down to his waist, and
encountering his hard, firm naked skin beneath the hem

of the shirt, she was brought to awareness of where they were once again headed. She pushed to separate them.

Adam let her go and turned away cursing under his breath. Eva watched him with consternation, somehow aware that he was being pushed beyond his own limits. But she was still confused, not fully understanding what was holding her back. Adam paced for a minute, a space of three or four feet, before stopping in front of her. He started to say something, then clamped his mouth closed. Eva watched him with concern. Finally he shook his head impatiently and turned away.

"Come on. We have to go back." And he went off through the ruins toward the Jeep with Eva behind him.

The Jeep pulled up on the familiar road below the house. They sat in silence when the engine was turned off, surrounded by summer darkness.

"Will—will you take the boat out tomorrow?" Eva's voice came quietly through the night air.

Adam shifted positions in the seat so that he was almost facing her. He bent his right elbow over the back of his seat. "I'm not sure. Would you come with me if I did?" he asked.

Eva sighed in a shaky little voice. "I don't know. I'm not sure if I should."

There was a long pause before he responded. "I know…"

Eva then gathered her things and climbed out of the Jeep. She was surprised when Adam followed.

"Eva…"

She turned to him. He walked over to her, towering over her, setting her pulse to race again.

"You aren't like Lavona Morris," he informed her distinctly. "And I won't treat you as if you are."

She didn't know how to respond to that. She lowered

her eyes nervously and shrugged. "Lavona is so—so beautiful. So sensual."

"So was my ex-wife," he said caustically.

Eva looked at his face in the dark. "But don't you like Lavona?"

Adam shifted from one foot to the other. "I like her well enough."

Eva frowned and pursed her lips ruefully. Adam could compare his ex-wife and Lavona. They were both beautiful. But he did not say the same of her. On the other hand, he'd said he wouldn't treat her as he did Lavona. She shook her head gently. There were too many differences for her to understand.

"Maxwell, why did you tell me that?" she asked softly.

"Because you're still not sure of me," he whispered, "or yourself."

She couldn't answer that because he was too close to the truth.

"Lavona and I understand each other. There's never been any pretending that our relationship was ever anything else outside of a bedroom."

Eva looked at him, somewhat in wonder. Did Adam see their relationship as anything more…or less…or different?

"Maxwell…I—I like you holding me." She felt the need to admit, to justify. He came closer to her and taking her by the shoulders turned her to face him fully. Adam stretched his fingers along one cheek, his thumb forcing her head up. He bent to kiss her gently, but thoroughly.

"That's a start," he said thickly. He turned back to his Jeep.

"Maxwell?"

He stopped and looked at her over his shoulder.

"Would you like to come upstairs?"

He hesitated only a second before answering. "No," he said firmly. "We both know what would happen if I do." He climbed into the Jeep, started the engine, and without another word drove away.

Eva climbed the stairs to her house. She put her things away in a slow, lethargic manner, thinking as she moved how the past seemed to be getting dimmer. And distantly unreal.

Chapter Seven

Eva lifted the rum drink absently and took a sip. She grimaced and put the glass down again, forcing the liquid in her mouth down her throat. The ice had melted in the glass, and the drink tasted like nothing more than warm, tinted water.

"I order you another one," Deacon said next to her.

"Oh, no. No more for me, thank you." Eva quickly inserted as Deacon moved to signal for the waiter.

"Come on, Eva," Deacon scoffed at her. "This is a celebration! It's Carnival time. Everybody drink and dance."

Eva smiled weakly, feeling a headache beginning to set in at her temples. "For me it's more fun just to watch. Maybe later," she assured him, hoping that later he would have forgotten. Deacon turned to have a word with his sister and brother-in-law, and Eva sighed inwardly, gently massaging her forehead.

The music being performed had a certain cadence and rhythm to it that at this moment seemed to be keeping exact step to the pain in her head. She closed her eyes for a moment, concentrating on blocking out one or the other and finding it didn't work.

Eva jumped guiltily at the voice in her ear, and the

arm which briefly rested around her back and shoulders. She turned her eyes back to Deacon.

"Good music, eh?" he flashed a wide smile from his dark face.

"Very nice," Eva agreed.

"They make love songs, you know," Deacon informed her.

Eva gave him a skeptical look. "It sounds too festive to be love songs."

"Oh yes. We like happy music for all things. Even sad occasions. We celebrate everything!" and he began to move his shoulders to the music in a sensual rotation, leaning toward her. Eva's eyes widened as they followed the suggestive movements. But then he laughed and grabbed for her hand. "That private dance," he whispered low, "only for lovers."

"Is it?" Eva asked wanly.

"Yes! I dance for you, yes? I dance the whole dance if you stay, marry Deacon."

Eva hoped her chuckle sounded like gentle amusement. "That's quite all right."

The musical evening had started with a steel band, which was lovely but just a bit too loud. Then it had changed to reggae for a while, complete with a lead singer in long Rastafarian dreadlocks. Now it was calypso, with everyone around her in the smoky room swaying to the music.

Eva looked at the crowd of people through the fog of cigarette smoke, at the mixture of people who'd come to celebrate the whole week on St. John. The streets and stores and restaurants had been hard pressed to accommodate not only those already on the island but those arriving from St. Thomas and Puerto Rico as well.

So far Eva had managed to avoid much of the crowds,

having spent the first half of the week in Adam Maxwell's company. The memory of those days made her want to be alone, apart from all of this celebration and merriment so that she could sort out her feelings. She had elected to avoid his company the previous day by deciding her cupboards were low on supplies and she had to shop in town to restock.

Eva had already spent two bad nights imagining Maxwell making love to her as Kevin stood in the background in censuring, hurt silence. The thought of Kevin had been effective in staying her and keeping her from Maxwell. But it had in no way stilled her desire or her need. What had settled instead was a kind of guilt and confusion-ladened depression. Part of it had to do with feeling as though she was afflicted with some inner energy, gravitating her closer and closer to the potent physical aura that was Maxwell. She felt herself opening up and responding to him in a way that, in her mind and admitted limited experience, could only be described as wanton. The other part of her depression was based on her growing knowledge that she wanted to experience all of it.

There was a charm and persuasive power to the man that went beyond the hard outer shell he so effectively wore for the rest of the world. But Eva was starting to feel that she was already reaching beneath the façade. Yet it had to happen slowly, so afraid was she of being sucked into a vortex of heated emotions that would destroy her.

On Wednesday morning Eva had driven to a small market just outside of Cruz Bay to do her shopping. It was as she stood in line at the checkout counter that she encountered the final link to set the depression firmly inside herself.

A thin little girl of about ten or eleven walked cautiously up to her and looked into her face shyly. Eva saw her staring and smiled in a friendly fashion. The little girl, who was very pretty with a heart-shaped caramel-colored face and enormous black eyes, returned the smile.

"Are you Diane's friend?" she asked Eva.

"Diane?" Eva questioned. "Oh you mean Diane Maxwell? Yes…I guess I am. Are you Dory?" Eva asked. Dory merely continued to stare at her and smile. "I understand you're in the parade on Friday?" Eva ventured comfortably.

"Uh-huh," was the response from Dory, apparently not inclined to be a conversationalist. "Diane helped me with my costume. Are you coming to see it?"

"I hope so." Eva looked around her. "Are you alone? Is Diane with you?"

"She went back to her father this morning."

"Oh, I see. But…"

"Dory is with me," came the sultry, lilting voice behind Eva. Her stomach churned as she twisted and recognized Lavona standing to the side. Lavona had her mass of thick wavy hair pulled back off her tawny face and pinned at the temples with combs. She wore an eyelet lace summer camisole, and it was obvious that she wore no bra with the flimsy top. She was well-built and proportioned, but Eva wondered that she had the nerve to be so blatant. The pretty top, however, did set off her creamy brown skin to perfection. It was worn with a pair of red slacks, molded to Lavona's legs and hips.

"Oh, hello," Eva mouthed politely, stiffening nonetheless with remembered anger at the way Lavona tended to treat her. Lavona didn't return the greeting, and Eva wondered in additional irritation if that was a habit she got from Adam, or he got from her.

Lavona looked at Eva's much less voluptuous form

with an expression that could easily be interpreted as one of derision and amusement. She gave the little girl, Dory, her packages. "I be right out. Stand outside now."

Dory took the packages. "See you on Friday," she said to Eva as she walked out of the store.

"Bye, Dory," Eva said to her retreating body. Eva took a deep breath and turned back to Lavona in curiosity. She found out at once that subtlety was not one of Lavona's strong points, either.

"Adam belongs to me, you know," she announced silkily.

Eva ground her teeth, hating to admit to herself that she loved the sound of this woman's voice. She wondered, ruefully, how Maxwell could refuse this beauty anything when she said his name with such allure.

"Does, er, he know this?" she asked Lavona blandly. Lavona's lashes swept low over her round cheeks, and her eyes were momentarily veiled.

"We've been together long time. He's very happy with me."

"I'm sure he is." Eva nodded, remembering Maxwell's blunt description of his relationship to this woman. "But I don't think he belongs to anyone."

"I just think you should know. He only wants one thing from you." Lavona laughed lightly then, and that too was musical. "He all the time tell me what women are good for."

"Maybe that's what you're good for," Eva interrupted angrily, "but he'd better not say so to me!"

Lavona arched a brow knowingly. "You like Adam, very much. You very foolish. He forget you before long. You go back home and he stay here with me."

Eva took a slow, deep breath to fill her lungs and steady her body. Her hands were clenched into tight angry fists in the pockets of her sweater. There was certainly probability in what Lavona was saying. Eva also realized that she herself had more or less admitted to an interest in Adam Maxwell that had slipped out spontaneously. "I think you're very foolish to let yourself be treated that way. Is that what you want?" she asked Lavona.

Lavona shrugged her shoulder negligently. Eva was fascinated. This woman might look soft and feminine, but she was tough and sure of herself. "I get from Adam what I want. He's very good-looking. All man, yes? But I won't stay with him forever. I am going to marry a rich man who can take care of me. I'll have pretty babies and a pretty home. Adam doesn't want that."

Eva raised her brows at Lavona's bold admission. "And I suppose you know what he does want?"

Lavona grimaced prettily. "Me…" she purred. "For now. And his fish."

It was not lost on Eva that in Lavona's mind, she apparently didn't compete on either level. She stared blankly at Lavona, and it suddenly hit her how ludicrous, how funny it was to be standing in a food market having this conversation over a man who was only just beginning to be more than a stranger, with a woman she didn't think very much of. Adam Maxwell could be much more to her. Did Lavona Morris actually see that in her? Could she be so much woman as to pick up on the dawning thoughts that she, Eva, may feel much more for Maxwell than made good sense? Florence Steward hadn't raised any fools, and Eva fervently hoped she wasn't going to disappoint her mother now.

"I'm sure you mean well," Eva said sarcastically to Lavona. "But I can take care of myself."

Lavona shrugged again. She didn't care one way or

the other. "Just so you don't think that Adam will. You be very sorry otherwise."

And with that Lavona turned and gracefully made her way from the store. Eva stood watching her departure for long minutes. Lavona had been very effective whether or not she knew it. If Eva was unsure before, she was now filled with more doubts and fears.

And even that afternoon as she met Deacon Butler and part of his family to attend the musical concert, Eva felt the mood persist, making it difficult for her to find a smile or to appear cheerful. She knew that she'd never have taken any of Lavona's speculations and observations to heart if there wasn't one or two truths in there somewhere.

Her depression settled in deeper. Eva tried to read the face of her watch. It was almost ten thirty. She let out a sigh of relief. Eva knew that the last ferry back to St. Thomas had been postponed until twelve o'clock. Deacon would be leaving soon, and she could go home to bed. Suddenly the music didn't seem so loud, and her headache was a low-grade throb she could live with for another hour or so.

Deacon's arm was across the back of her chair, his rough, callused fingers occasionally patting her arm. He was a nice man, but she hoped he didn't think that anything more would develop from this casual evening. Eva liked him very much, but certainly not more than that.

Eva turned her head in his direction, and her eyes caught a familiar body and face. Her eyes lifted and she found herself looking into the closed, hard gaze of Adam Maxwell. Beside him, looking exotic and lovely, was Lavona Morris.

Eva's stomach sank somewhere around her knees and her heart lurched to her throat. Adam was dressed in wheat-colored slacks and a short-sleeved black cotton shirt opened at the throat. The smoky haze of the room cast an eerie light and shadow over his features for a moment, so that his jaw and sensuous bottom lip seemed prominently outlined. Eva felt a familiar constriction in her chest at the sight of him. But Adam's eyes swept briefly over her and away without any greeting or acknowledgment as Lavona claimed his attention with a slender hand to his arm.

Lavona was dressed in a clinging black dress with spaghetti straps. It had slits up the sides and was cinched at the waist with a gold belt. With a hand at the back of her waist, Adam urged Lavona to the other side of the room and a vacant table. Lavona was lost to Eva's view through the crowds of heads in front of her, but Adam's shoulders and head were clearly discernable above everyone else, even as he slouched in his seat, an ankle lifted across his bent knee, very like the first time she'd seen him.

A wave of inadequacy washed over her at once but it was more an indication of her own state of mind than it was of her physical attractiveness. Eva wore a taupe crepe dress, shirred at the shoulders. It had a mock wrap front that showed suggestively the deep valley of her breasts. It had a slim skirt to it and was also belted with a black crepe sash. While Lavona's dress was obviously displaying her charms, Eva's subtly hinted at hers, presenting a much more enticing picture.

"You ready for another drink?" Deacon crooned in her ear, causing Eva to jump. His fingers rubbed the ball of her shoulder and a chill shook her that had nothing to do with the touch but rather with the apparent aloof indifference Adam had shown her seconds before. Had he completely wiped Monday and Tuesday from his mind? Was Lavona right about him?

"Yes, please," Eva murmured.

"What would you like?"

She shook her head and shrugged. "Anything…"

She ended up having two more drinks and her head began to pound again. Deacon tried to persuade her to dance, but Eva firmly refused. She was continually drawn to Maxwell's direction, but he seemed totally engulfed in either the music or Lavona. But in the following noise, movements, and music, Eva missed that he covertly watched her, too.

Finally at eleven forty-five, Deacon, his sister, and brother-in-law rose to leave. Deacon kept a possessive arm about Eva's shoulder, and she smiled at him, determined to leave Maxwell's presence with equal indifference. The still night air was welcomed after the long hours inside the closed and stuffy restaurant hall.

"I take you home now," Deacon said.

"No, don't. That's not necessary," Eva said quickly.

"Yeah, can't have you travelin' in the dark by yourself."

"That's sweet of you, but there are too many people around for anything to happen to me. Besides, you'll miss the last ferry," Eva reasoned. That finally sank in.

Eva walked with them to the ferry and watched them board. She was not surprised when Deacon gave her a quick affectionate kiss on the cheek and left her. She smiled sadly.

"You come to St. Thomas again next week, yes?" he shouted at her from the ferry.

"Maybe!" She waved as the boat slipped slowly from the dock.

"Then I come back here!"

Eva laughed at the wide grin he gave her. "Good-night!" she shouted as the engines began to rev. Then she walked to her Jeep for the short ride home.

Eva was emotionally exhausted, but unable to fall asleep. She tossed and turned in the bed for more than an hour, until the sheets were warmed from her body and uncomfortable. She climbed out of bed and went to take a quick, cool shower. She came out and toweled herself dry, prepared to try and sleep. But Eva stopped in mid action when there came the sound of footsteps on her gallery. Her heart thudded in terror, suddenly aware of her total isolation and vulnerability. Silently she reached for her silk kimono-styled robe and wrapped it quickly around her still-damp body. In the dark she tiptoed to the door connecting the gallery to her room.

"Who is it?" she asked softly through the dark. The footsteps shifted, and a light was turned on causing Eva to blink painfully. Adam Maxwell stood in the glaring brightness, scowling at her. He quickly took in her scanty attire. Adam pushed his hands into his trouser pockets and leaned against the wall, his rugged brown face oddly shadowed by the ceiling light.

"Are you alone?" he asked.

The question took her by surprise, but just for an instant Eva was tempted to prevaricate. Instead, she asked her own question. "Why do you want to know?" She leaned in the bedroom doorway, pulling the robe belt tighter around her waist. Maxwell's eyes, somewhat overly bright, dropped to the movement and then slowly raised back to her face. It was hard for Eva to decide what look he wore now.

"I wouldn't want to, er, interrupt anything," he said sarcastically.

Eva let out a sigh of impatience. "The only thing

you're interrupting is my sleep. Do you realize it's almost two o'clock?'' Another thought quickly entered her mind, wiping away her defensive posture. ''Where's Diane?'' she asked, frowning.

Maxwell was still watching her in an odd way.

''Diane is home. Dory Hamilton is staying with her tonight.''

''And Lavona? Is she staying with you?'' Eva asked before she could stop herself, because the thought that she might be right was suddenly so disturbing. She saw a sparkle, a light of challenge flash in Adam's eyes. Eva bit down on the inside of her bottom lip and moved to sit at the glass and wrought-iron dining table. ''What do you want?'' she asked quietly, looking at him, but keeping her eyes low, somewhere around his chest and the opening of his shirt.

There was a pause, and slowly Maxwell came away from the wall and walked over to where she sat. Eva had the strangest sensation of being stalked by a predatory animal, stealthily moving upon her without making a sound.

''I saw Milly Decker tonight. She asked about you.''

Eva looked up. She realized now that Maxwell had been drinking. And although the words he spoke were clear and understandable, they were heavy and slow.

''She said she had something to return to you.'' As he talked, Adam slowly took his hand out of his pocket and threw something on the table in front of Eva. It was her worn red wallet.

Eva stared at it blankly for a moment.

''It was turned into the tourist office a few days ago on St. Thomas. All the money is gone, of course, but your ID and pictures are probably still there.''

Eva raised her eyes to his. He was frowning at her,

and her almond-shaped eyes were questioning. But Adam continued to talk.

"I told Milly I'd see that you got it back. Her business card was inside, so it was sent back to her office first."

Eva realized by the inflection in Adam's voice that he'd looked through the contents of the wallet himself. He'd discovered the money gone and looked at all her pictures…all of her history. Those of Gail as a baby and a wedding picture of her and Kevin. A picture taken by her mother at one of Gail's birthday parties of the three of them together. Adam had looked into the very heart of what used to be her life. Eva hadn't felt so vulnerable in a long time. Maxwell knew everything there was to know about her now.

She absently opened and flipped through the wallet, watching familiar cards, pictures, tickets, whiz past her view in their familiar places. "Thank you," she said in a very low voice, closing and snapping the wallet shut. There followed a long silence in which she didn't look at Adam.

"Why didn't you say something?" Adam asked quietly, his deep voice nonetheless resounding in the open space. It was tightly controlled, disguising an emotion that Eva did not recognize because she was not used to Adam expressing it. "Why didn't you tell me I was wrong about all those things I said…stop me from making a fool of myself?"

"You did that all by yourself," Eva corrected softly. "At the time I didn't want your sympathy. We didn't know each other. Kevin and Gail were—were my own personal hurt. There was nothing you could say or not say to change that, Maxwell."

Then she did look at him, determined to keep the sudden swelling of emotions and tears down. "My sorrow belongs to me and…I didn't want to share it then."

Adam didn't respond, but still frowned, his jaw working tensely. "You've really been through a lot…" There was a degree of admiration and respect in the way he phrased it. "You even look different. That is you in the picture, isn't it?"

She nodded silently.

Adam slowly walked the length of the gallery and stood for a while looking out into the night all alone. Then he retraced his steps back to her. Eva never moved. The sudden silence locked them together in the narrow gallery. Adam reached her and continued to sweep over her with his troubled eyes, as if there were suddenly a dozen things about her he hadn't seen before. When he spoke again, it was completely off the subject at hand. It threw Eva off guard, but she was grateful for the change to something else.

"So…was that your, er, cabdriver from St. Thomas?" he asked.

Eva sat straighter in her chair, lifting her chin defensively. "His name is Deacon," she informed him clearly. "Yes. That's him. He's been very nice to me."

"I bet he has," Adam drawled, his words again sounding thick.

"I don't like what you're implying," Eva said haughtily.

"Are you telling me that…Deacon hasn't come on to you? Hasn't made the big play?"

"No, he hasn't."

"Then he must be slow. You know he wants to…"

Eva scoffed softly. "You mean like you? If I didn't know you better, I'd say you were jealous!"

Adam went livid. His jaw tightened and his eyes were

dark and stormy. Eva involuntarily sat way back in her chair when he braced both hands on the table in front of her, leaning forward. "I don't think there's any comparison…"

"I'm not likely to make that mistake! Deacon is a kind, sweet man. I can't compare you to him," she informed him angrily, striking back in any way that would get to him. She didn't like his high-handed way with her, when she had no idea if he cared anything for her. It would have been different if he was expressing some real concern, but she knew Adam wanted one thing from her. Hadn't Lavona said so?

"And I don't want to be compared to Lavona!" she blurted out in rising indignation, coming to her feet abruptly. Her nerves, feelings, and confusions were positively raw at the moment, and she ranted mostly out of a need to just release some of the anxiety. Since Adam Maxwell was indirectly the cause for most of it, she made him the target.

Adam stared at her for a moment and then threw out his arms in a gesture of exasperation. "What the hell does Lavona have to do with this?" he stormed at her.

"We both know what she wants from you, too! From any man for that matter. You have no right to assume that I am after a man for similar reasons! I was married to a wonderful man that no one can replace!"

"Do you think Deacon's serious?"

"Maybe he is. What do you care? Anyway, I don't intend to see him again. I—I don't want to encourage him." Eva was starting to shake. She hugged herself and turned away from Adam. She wanted him to hold her…not yell at her that way.

"You've returned my wallet. You can go now. Back to Lavona's waiting arms, for all I care! Just—just leave me alone.'' Her voice threatened to break. But Adam was in no state either to recognize what she was experiencing or needed.

Adam clicked his teeth impatiently, sighing deeply behind her. ''I haven't slept with Lavona since the day of Diane's accident.''

The confession surprised Eva, and she looked cautiously over her shoulder at him. ''You don't have to tell me that. It's not my business.''

''But it bothers you, doesn't it?''

''What does it matter?''

Adam came to stand in front of her. He took her by the upper arms and shook her slightly. ''It matters to me, dammit! Tell me!''

Eva gasped at his reaction. She could smell the warm vapor of alcohol on his breath, and he was not as steady as he'd first seemed. His fingers were pressed almost painfully into her arms, but she made no move to free herself.

''You're—you're both so indifferent! You don't care about her, and she doesn't care about you. You're both just...using each other!''

Adam's frown deepened, and his eyes seemed distant and glazed. ''And you're not used to that, are you? You're used to, what...tenderness? Respect? Love? Grow up, Eva. That's not always possible.''

Her chin began to quiver with the truth of his words. She knew he was right. But that still didn't change need, desire, wanting to be held and touched. His hands gentled their grasp and were warm on her skin. ''Maybe not. You'd know better than I would. But...should I accept anything less?'' Eva's eyes almost pleaded with him. She remembered Tuesday so well and the time on the sand of that little cove. She could so easily recall the feel of his hands, mouth, and body.

Adam's eyes swept over her in puzzlement as he felt her trembling. But he only let out an exhausted sigh and released her. "No...I guess you couldn't. Not you," he responded. Adam sat down heavily on the sofa and tilted his head back against the cushion. "You have to do what feels right to you. We all do."

Eva moved slowly nearer to him. "And you don't care that it's like that? Don't you want more than that?"

"Eva, more than that is a responsibility. Sometimes it wipes you out. Leaves you cold. You know what I mean?"

Eva's body slumped in defeat. "Yes...I know what you mean."

They were quiet for a long time, Eva watching him, trying to glean further understanding from him, of him. He closed his eyes. Eva wondered at his anger and vehemence and could attach no explanation to their arguing. She did notice the tired look to his face and furrowing of his brow.

"I'll make some coffee," Eva offered. Adam merely nodded absently.

In the kitchen her hands did the mechanical chore, while her mind and heart warred with each other. Her mind could reason, argue, fight with him about right or wrong or indifference. But her heart only knew desire. Adam was like no one she'd ever met before, perhaps someone she shouldn't really know, could not hope to get next to. But she was drawn to him dangerously, like a moth to the bright orange and yellows of a candle flame. She could get hurt...badly burned...but all the arguments in the world weren't going to change the way he made her feel. So far Adam had only touched on it, barely brought it to life. And Eva hoped that if it was allowed to be fully realized, that she wouldn't sink beneath the tide of feelings and lose herself.

She carried two cups of black coffee to the gallery. Maxwell was very still.

"Maxwell?" She called his name softly. There was no answer, and his even, deep breathing told her he was asleep.

Eva put his cup down on the table and sitting in a chair facing him, watched Adam thoughtfully as she sipped at her coffee. It suddenly dawned on Eva that this man had his own deep hurts and disappointments. She was not the only one to have survived a personal loss. Granted, hers was more tragic by its occurrence, but was his any less painful to him?

She got up and lightly touched his shoulder, and once again called his name. Adam's head gently rolled to the side away from her, and he slept on. Eva sighed and chewed her lip in indecision. She was aware that Diane and Dory were alone in the house down the road. But it was not so far from Dory's parents, and so she figured that they'd probably be okay. Eva lightly spread the afghan over Adam's chest and arms, and went back to her room to her own bed.

It was much later when she again heard sounds in the night. It was almost like rain, but it seemed to be falling on only one part of the house. The sound completely awakened her, and her sleep-fogged brain fought to locate it. Eva opened her eyes and saw that the light from the gallery was still on.

The sound stopped, and a moment later, Maxwell stepped from the bathroom shower, toweling himself. He was quiet and moved slowly, and Eva knew that if the shower itself hadn't woken her, he would have tried to finish without her knowing.

Eva rolled halfway onto her back facing him, a thin sheet for cover pulled just over her chest. Seeing Adam across the room, she hugged the sheet closer to her nakedness. Not since her first week had she worn a nightgown to bed, discovering that she woke in the morning drenched in sweat from too much covering.

Adam stopped his toweling at the movements from the bed. He looked in her direction. "I woke up covered in sweat from that damned thing you put over me," he rumbled in his resonant voice. Eva said nothing. She was too cognizant of the fact that Adam stood naked only a few feet from her. It was too dark in the room to distinguish any more detail than his outline, the movement of his arms with the towel, and the mass of dark hair on his broad chest.

"You should have sent me home. I drank too much."

"Yes, I know. I tried to," her voice came, a mere whisper, disembodied in the dark.

"Did I get obnoxious?"

"Yes," she said honestly. Adam grunted.

Then she knew that Adam was moving toward her where she lay in the large bed alone. Some warning flashed through her, some innate sense of the order of events told her what was about to happen. Her heart skipped beats in sudden agitation, and there was a fluttering of nerves in her stomach. But she never moved, and she said no more. It was an overwhelming provocative and tantalizing feeling to lie and wait for him to reach her.

Adam towered over her, and then he slowly dropped the towel to the floor. Eva's breath caught in her chest. He lowered his frame to the side of the bed, and it dipped gently under the weight. Eva tried to see his eyes. They would tell her all she wanted to know in this moment of discovery, but they were hidden by the dark.

One of Adam's hands reached over her body and braced on the bed. The other came up to search out the smooth contours of her face, gently. He located her lips and with his thumb, separated her lips, and pressed it against the lower rim of small white teeth. "You should have sent me home..." he repeated in a thick voice, as if he was placing the blame on her for anything that now took place.

Then the hand at her mouth came down to locate the top of the sheet covering her and pulled it away. Adam couldn't see her any better than she could him, but he easily located her breast and cupped his hand warmly, completely over one. The touch immediately evoked a chill through her as the hand was cool from the shower water. He squeezed the breast gently while she lay there unresisting, but under his hand he could detect the increase in her breathing. Maxwell's fingers played gently and sensuously with the nipple of her breast. A warm languid sensation of delight and longing washed over Eva, and she knew she wanted this. She did nothing to stop him.

When she didn't move to object, Adam leaned forward to brush a warm, openmouthed kiss over her lips.

"I want to make love to you," he whispered low with a kind of urgency that Eva was at once susceptible to. One of her hands came up to brush over the thick soft top of his head. It was both a possessive and comforting move, and Adam took his signal from it. They may sometimes have been emotional antagonists in the light, but in the intimate darkness of her bedroom, they now both wanted the same thing.

Not another word was spoken as Maxwell lifted the sheet away completely and moved onto the bed with her. Eva shivered once, almost violently, and a sigh escaped her parted lips as Maxwell shifted again to lie gently, full length upon her. He was a big man, but his weight was not uncomfortable on her. Eva raised her arms to his shoulder and Maxwell bowed his head to find her mouth and kiss her.

Eva gave up the struggle of indecision. She wanted to be here with him. She thought not of the past or even of the future but allowed herself to just enjoy and experience the moment. She was beside herself with a rising desire and passion that was totally unlike anything she'd ever known before. It nagged and pulled at her insides, sending swirls of tension throughout her loins, and she gave herself up to it.

She answered his kisses, his touch with her own. She savored the taste and texture of his tongue, the feel of his firm lips. She enjoyed and was excited by the pressing and rubbing of the furry mat of his chest on her sensitive breasts.

Eva was not sure what to do, but Maxwell was not reticent. He was bold, but he was also surprisingly tender. Eva was unaware of the tears of relief that rolled unchecked down her cheek and into her hairline as Maxwell caressed her fevered body with knowledgeable gentleness.

After a short time there was no hesitation on Eva's part, and when he stroked her thigh, she responded. He moved slowly upon her, groaning softly in his total intimate possession of her. Their movements together became slow and rhythmic. For what seemed an eternity…and then not long enough.

Each new feeling and tension built upon the old until

there didn't seem to be any place for it all to go. Their
movements matched, becoming more exact and demanding. Eva felt a fullness within, she felt like an opened
flower basking in the life-giving forces of a more omnip-
otent power. They held tightly together.

Flashes of colored lights burst behind Eva's eyelids
and blood seemed to rush hotly to her head. She panted
into his shoulder, calling his name. Eva was overcome.
She hadn't expected it to be like this. So…satisfying, and
complete.

Then Adam at last raised his head to search her face.
Eva's eyes were still closed, her breathing still softly hurried. He kissed her, and there was the faint taste of lingering alcohol on his tongue. Something in the way he
kissed her told Eva that for Adam this moment was more
than he'd expected as well.

She still couldn't bring herself to look at Adam as she
settled down from the most delicious sensual storm she'd
ever known. Her body and responses belonged to someone else, a new Eva Duncan. She'd never been so abandoned with Kevin, and she'd loved him dearly. And she
was also experiencing the inevitable shame and guilt.
What must Adam be thinking of her, that he'd had no
resistance to break down, no trouble issuing arousal and
response that shook her from head to toe.

Eva couldn't tell what Adam was thinking, but he
moved his head to rub his hard jaw along her cheek and
to nuzzle in the furrow between her neck and shoulder.
He smelled of healthy male sweat again and summer
heat. He smelled of passion and virility, and she was
intoxicated all over again.

"Eva…I can't believe how soft you feel," he mumbled into her skin. A large damp hand slid up her thigh,
causing the sensitive skin to quiver, up to her waist and

rib cage to her small firm breasts. He moved the palm of his hand over the curved surface and there was an immediate response in the soft brown peak. "Not just your mouth, but...all over." He kissed her neck, dragged his mouth to kiss a rounded shoulder. "Ummmmm...I like having you in my bed with me..."

Eva voluntarily lifted her chin as his mouth sorted out the hollow of her throat and kissed it, too.

"This is my bed, Maxwell," she reminded him in a whisper. She could feel him chuckle, his body shaking.

"A minor detail..." Suddenly he sobered. His eyes swept over her features, and a hand brushed over her cheeks where her tears had dried. "Are you sorry, Eva? Are you still afraid?"

Eva's small hands slid up his smooth muscled back to push her fingers into the tight curls of the hair on his nape. "No, Max, I'm not," she said to both his questions.

Adam captured her mouth, kissing her deeply, and never having separated from her before, now filled her again. They rocked and swayed, whispered and murmured to each other, receiving one another poignantly until they were once again helpless victims of a sweet, aching need for release.

Chapter Eight

Eva used the soft bristles of her hairbrush to fluff up the short, looped curls at her temple. She had endured rollers in order to style her hair today in soft curls, giving her face an over-all gentle appearance, a breezy carefree look. She wore a pair of wide-legged hot-pink walking shorts, which looked more like a short skirt on her slender body, and a lavender blouse with capped sleeves and a stand-up mandarin collar. It was a bright and cheerful combination to match her mood.

Eva touched a mascara wand to her lashes, added a blusher to the high rounded points of her cheeks, and some lip gloss. She gave one final flick to a curl with a finger, and put small gold-ball earrings into her pierced ears.

Out on the gallery she finished a glass of orange juice and looked out on the beautiful morning, wondering why everything seemed so clear, so bright, so new today. Of course, she knew the answer. It had nothing to do with the beautiful day, since all of the days had been the same since her arrival. It had to do with herself. She was different. In the dark last night, in Adam Maxwell's arms, Eva had let go of Kevin and the past and had gone in search of and found new facets of herself. It had been exhilarating.

After making love a second time, Maxwell had just held her quietly in his embrace, his arms around her, her head tucked under his chin against his chest and throat, and one of his muscular legs thrown over her thigh and hip. They didn't sleep and they didn't talk. Eva was glad that Maxwell didn't have anything to say, as words would have broken the magic aura they'd created for the moment. Just touching each other seemed adequate communication.

The sky was turning gray and morning sounds broke the night-long silence when Maxwell sighed deeply and released Eva, climbing out of the bed. The bed now seemed enormous and very empty to Eva. Maxwell stood magnificent and larger than life before her, his rich brown body sinewy and flexing away the night. Adam bent to kiss her quickly and turned to stride to retrieve his clothing. He came back not three minutes later, fully dressed. He sat on the edge of the bed, one hand braced next to her head.

"I don't want Diane to wake up and not find me there," he said in a deep whisper, with a hint of regret that he had to leave her.

Eva nodded. "Of course not. Go on…it's almost light."

But he sat looking at her in the half light, his eyes searching over her face. "Today's the parade for Carnival. We're going down to Cruz Bay around eleven. Are you going?"

"I'd planned to…"

He hesitated. "Why not come with us. Diane hasn't seen you for a few days. She's bound to ask about you."

Eva half smiled at his using Diane for an excuse. It

made her wonder about the other times Adam might have hidden his true motives behind his daughter. "If you want me to," Eva responded evenly.

Adam nodded. "Yes...I want you to." But he continued to sit. He opened his mouth to say something else, and Eva, half guessing that it might concern the night they'd just spent together, forestalled him.

"Maxwell, go...it'll be light soon."

He touched her cheek. "Okay. Be ready by eleven?"

"I will."

"Now get some sleep..." And then he got up and left quietly, moving through the gallery and out of the house. The ignition of his Jeep engine was a startling sound in the dawn air.

Eva lay thoughtful for a moment, then ran her hand slowly down the space that he had recently occupied. She rolled in that direction on her side and was promptly asleep.

Now as she finished the juice and continued to scan the bright horizon, she had a sudden sobering thought. She had not actually changed at all, and neither had Maxwell. It was just that something new had happened to both of them together. Eva couldn't help wondering if Lavona Morris was right in her evaluation of Adam. Had Eva just been a conquest last night? And she also wondered if Adam was ever as careful with Lavona as she felt he'd been with her in their lovemaking, except near the end when the full force of his virility had swept over her, thrust into her. What was it about the experience that had her examining it with curiosity and with less guilt than she'd thought would be there at her betrayal of Kevin? And it nagged at her mind and conscience that Adam might still return to his amorous liaison with Lavona. Eva wasn't sure it mattered…which was not the same as not caring.

Eva was fully aware of the contradiction she was in, having informed Adam that she didn't want to be treated with the indifference he showed Lavona. But that did not mean necessarily that she would reject his overtures and not respond to them. She sighed. It was much more complicated than her experiences had ever given her to understand. She recognized as well that she wasn't indifferent to him, and her lovemaking with Adam had, by no means, been casual to her. Eva puzzled then, over where the relationship would go from here, what would happen next.

In all the time Eva had been in the house, the phone had never once sounded. Its sudden ringing trilled through the gallery space, startling her with the noise. It began to ring a second time before she broke out of her reverie and hurried to answer.

"Hello?"

"Hi, Eva. Milly Decker…"

"Hi, Milly. How are you?"

"Oh, pretty good. Getting ready to go down to the parade like everyone else on the island, no doubt," the woman chuckled with humor. "I'm calling to find out if you'd like to meet me and watch it?"

"That's nice of you to ask, but…I—I was already invited."

"Oh!" Milly exclaimed surprised. "If I'm not being nosy, by whom?"

Eva frowned for a moment, thinking. She didn't want to put the wrong emphasis on the fact that she was going with Adam Maxwell and his daughter. Adam was right. St. John was a very small island, and people who knew him must know of his connection to Lavona.

"With Adam Maxwell and his daughter Diane," Eva finally supplied.

"Oh, fine. By the way, did Adam return your wallet to you?"

"Yes, he did, thank you. I was surprised to get it. I thought it was gone forever."

"Well I'm glad for you it wasn't. It's such a pain having to replace ID. It was good of Adam to offer and return it. I didn't realize you two had finally met."

"Oh, er, well, I've been sailing with him…and Diane," Eva quickly added. But warm blood went rushing to her neck and face at the remembrance of her lone sail with Adam and their short, but exquisite, foray on the beach.

"Isn't sailing fun? I'm so glad you got a chance to go. Did you enjoy it?"

Eva smiled softly. "Very much," she admitted.

"Well…since you seem all taken care of this afternoon, how about having dinner with me tomorrow night? Nothing fancy, just a few friends. Anna Simpson, the public relations director for the local tourist board, will be there. She was born here but went to school in Chicago. I think you'll enjoy meeting her. And there'll be Margot Levine, who directs the high school steel band…it should be fun."

"I'd love to come," Eva responded, delighted.

"Good, good. It might be a late evening. Get a few of us together and we talk a lot!" Milly laughed. "You're not afraid to drive back late alone, are you?"

"No, not at all."

"All right then!"

Mildred Decker gave her driving directions and soon Eva replaced the phone in its cradle. Eva smiled ruefully, remembering Milly Decker telling her the day she arrived that the orders from Martin Isaacs were that Milly take care of Eva. Still it was fun having something to do that wouldn't put her in close proximity to Adam.

Eva was rinsing out her juice glass when her name was called.

"Eva! Are you ready?" Diane bounded through the entrance, her arms in the air as she grappled with her loose hair. She wore a yellow dress that buttoned down the front and stopped just above her knees.

Eva smiled at the little girl, noting at once that Diane had lost some weight in the last week and was looking taller and more trim. "Hello, Diane. I haven't seen you in so long."

"I was very busy," Diane informed Eva with some show of importance.

"So I heard. Helping Dory with her costume…"

Diane nodded, as she twisted and struggled with her hair. Eva shook her head at Diane's effort.

"Would you like me to do that for you?" she asked as she moved from the kitchen and directed Diane to sit at the dining table.

Diane kept up a running stream of talk about what she'd been doing all week. And then she got suddenly quiet. Eva tipped her head forward to see Diane's frowning face.

"What's the matter?" Eva asked as she combed Diane's hair off her face. She pulled it all back to the top of Diane's head, off-centered it into a soft bun, and secured it with hairpins.

Diane sighed and pouted out her lower lip. "I go home tomorrow…"

"Oh…is it time already?" Eva asked.

"Yeah," Diane answered, obviously disappointed.

Eva sat down next to her. "Did you have a good time while you were here?"

"Oh, yeah. It was my favorite time. I told Daddy I didn't want to go home."

"What did he say to that?"

"He said I didn't have to go if I didn't want to."

Eva frowned. "Then why go tomorrow? Why not stay a few weeks more?"

Diane slumped back in her chair and began to swing her foot. "'Cause I'm supposed to go to my grandmother's house with my mother and stepfather."

"Oh...I'm sorry," Eva said with sympathy.

Diane brightened a little. "But Daddy said I could come for Christmas if I wanted to."

"Did he?" Eva responded, happy with Adam's understanding of the situation.

Diane nodded sagely. "He said I could stay the whole holiday!"

Eva felt a flood of warm gratitude and admiration for Maxwell's decision. He and Diane had come a long way together in two weeks. "I'm very pleased for you, Diane."

"And you know what else?"

"No, what?"

"Look what he gave me!" Diane lifted her leg, and frowning, Eva's eye followed the length of the brown limb, but saw nothing unusual. "Look...look!" Diane said impatiently and began wiggling her toes. Something flashed and Eva picked up the glint of gold on a delicate, very thin band daintily circling one of Diane's toes.

Eva smiled and raised a brow. "It's very pretty. But don't you have it on the wrong part of your body?"

"Uh?" Diane puzzled.

"The ring is supposed to be on your finger."

"Oh no!" Diane giggled. "It's a toe ring! Everyone has one. Dory has one. And so does Lavona," she grimaced, rolling her eyes heavenward.

"I've never heard of that before," Eva confessed.

"It's special. They only wear them here on St. John."

"I see," Eva murmured in amusement, seeing how grown-up Diane sounded.

"Ooooh! I almost forgot!" Diane jumped to her feet with an exclamation. "Daddy's waiting for us. We better hurry or he'll leave us!" She ran for the steps.

Eva grabbed her camera, glasses, and purse and hurried after Diane. She suggested they drive her Jeep to save time. Eva bent quickly before climbing into the vehicle to pick a wild hibiscus along the house wall. Once in the Jeep, she leaned over and attached it to the side of Diane's topknot. The effect was winsome and pretty. Diane ooohed her image in the rearview mirror, occasionally touching the flower during the short ride, as if to make sure it was still there.

Diane went running into the house calling her father, and Eva followed. She was pleasantly surprised to find the house clean and neat, magazines and books stacked or shelved, and all of Adam's specimens confined to one part of the room instead of all over the place.

"Daddy! Look what Eva did!" Diane yelled. Adam emerged from his room, pulling a blue shirt down over the waist of a pair of white summer slacks.

Adam braced his hands on his hips and let out a low wolf whistle at his daughter as she paraded her hairstyle in front of him.

"Oh, Daddy!" Diane scoffed with embarrassment, but nonetheless happily as she moved to put her arms around his waist in a hug. Adam pulled Diane to himself with his arm and, smiling, bent to kiss the top of her head.

Then Adam raised his head and his light brown eyes connected with Eva, as she stood for a moment watching father and daughter. She smiled tentatively, and although Adam said nothing, his look said that he thanked her for the attention given to Diane and also that he was remembering their last time together, as he ran his eyes over her lithesome, pert outfit.

Cruz Bay's main street was lined with people waiting for the start of the parade, which finally began nearly two hours late. Apparently that was traditional, too.

Adam found a conveniently large shade tree for them to stand under at the beginning of the parade route. Participants in costumes strolled in happy groups to take their place in the procession. Eva used a whole roll of film even before the parade got started. She caught a nice image of Adam leaning nonchalantly against the tree with Diane leaning back against him. Both were looking off in the same direction watching the practicing members of a band. In the instant Eva saw the remarkable similarity between father and daughter. Eva took a picture and one more as Adam put his hand on Diane's shoulder and bent forward to say something into her ear.

Eva had a picture in her own mind now of them together that showed her a Maxwell much more at ease with his daughter, concerned about her, enjoying her company, and happy to have her with him. He'd discovered being a father again, and Eva was emotionally moved and pleased for him.

Adam looked suddenly in her direction and gave her a quizzical look as she stood with her camera poised in one hand. "What are you doing with that thing? Not taking my picture, I hope," he said caustically. "I won't take responsibility if your camera breaks!"

Eva laughed at him. "You do and I'll get the Mocko Jumbies after you!" she quipped.

Adam looked in surprise at her. "What do you know about Mocko Jumbies?"

Eva found herself hesitating. "I—I know that they're supposed to chase away evil spirits and protect you. Deacon Butler told me about them," she added reluctantly. Then she watched as a shadow dropped and his mouth pursed. Adam nodded indifferently and turned away again.

Eva's smile slowly faded. She didn't understand why it bothered him that she knew Deacon. She sighed helplessly and advanced the film in her camera. Off in the distance was the sound of bugles and drums. There was a whistle blast, a moment's pause, and the bugles and drums broke into a march introduction that heralded the start of the parade.

Eva took up a position on the road edge that allowed her to see the procession and take pictures. The crowd began to swell and crush together in a bunch. Some rather impetuous teenaged boys, jockeying for a better view, elbowed Eva aside, and she found herself at their backs, unable to see. She lost sight of Adam and Diane, and in frustration, looked for a small opening somewhere else that would allow her to get through.

A large hand grabbed for hers, and she turned her head to find Adam pulling her away from the crowd and farther down the road. They caught up to Diane who was standing clapping in excitement and trying to catch the goodies being thrown from the passing floats.

Adam pulled Eva in front of him, and his large body protected her from the jostling and maintained for her a clear view of the rest of the parade.

Dory floated by dressed in a white lacy dress and wearing a tiara, having been chosen a crowned princess for the day. Diane waved and shouted furiously, until Adam had to whisper to her to calm down. Which she did, but only for a moment.

The crowd began to close in again, but Adam maintained his stance, putting a hand possessively on Eva's waist. His touch seemed to burn through her clothing to her skin. And she was not surprised to realize that she enjoyed his sudden personal care of her. And then Adam moved closer until her back was against his chest and thighs. Eva held her breath. She stole a glance over her shoulder at him but his attention seemed to be momentarily focused on the proceedings of the parade. Eva was very conscious of his firm body so close to her and began to feel also giddy with the aura of his masculinity.

Eva forced herself to concentrate and pay attention as Diane pointed out one of Dory's brothers playing in a drum corp and the other who was one of the Mocko Jumbies, walking gracefully on six-foot stilts and dressed in gaily patterned pants and top. She was impressed with his agility and daring on the long, thin poles. And then the parade was over.

Diane asked to go with Dory to the school to help her undress from her fancy outfit. Adam agreed, saying he'd pick her up there in a few hours. Then Adam and Eva proceeded to trail behind everyone else into town. All over there was music and spontaneous dancing in the streets as the locals celebrated. It was even more crowded now, Adam again took firm hold of her hand as they walked leisurely.

Eva loved the secure feel of his grip and the feeling that they belonged together. It was surprising how everyone else noticed and, respectful of their connection, walked around instead of between them. But they soon got tired of the crowds and moved off to the less populated side streets. They found a bench near the main square. Adam purchased frothy piña coladas to sip as they sat and people-watched. Eva was feeling a contentment that had long been absent in her life. Adam watched her happy face thoughtfully. Then he reached out to flick a curl with his index finger and raised a brow seductively at her.

"I didn't get any sleep this morning, you know," he said hoarsely.

"That's too bad. I did," Eva came back, looking at him impertinently. Adam grunted.

"I thought I'd get a quick nap for an hour or so. But I got in and Diane and Dory were up a half hour later. They made me breakfast," he informed her in a low voice deep with surprise and pleasure.

Eva tilted her head and looked closely at him. "Diane says she goes home tomorrow."

Adam frowned slightly. He brushed a leaf off the leg of his pants, the brown of his arm contrasting against the white fabric. "That's right. I have to get her over to St. Thomas by two o'clock."

Eva absently used her straw to dig for the cherry in the bottom of her cup. "She says she's coming down for Christmas."

"Yeah, that's right," he confirmed casually.

"You like having her with you, don't you?" Eva asked softly after a small pause.

Adam slouched on the bench a little and crossed an ankle over a bent knee. One arm rested on the bench ledge behind Eva's back. He turned his head to stare at her but didn't answer her question directly. Instead, he looked out over the busy street, squinted into the bright water reflected with sunlight beyond the harbor.

"You know what she told me? She says I don't take good care of myself. She says it's a good thing she comes down once a year to check up on me!"

Eva laughed softly to herself. "Do you think she's right?"

He shrugged. "Probably." Adam shot her a quick look with a quirked brow. "And despite what you may think of me, I really do try when she comes down to do the right thing."

Eva played idly with her now-empty cup. "I'm sure you do, Maxwell."

"Having Diane stay with me…makes everything different. Do you know what I mean?"

She nodded. Adam looked once more toward the harbor.

"She made me breakfast this morning. A couple of nights ago it was dinner."

"How was it?" Eva asked curiously. Maxwell paused, pursing his lips.

"Interesting," he said tactfully. Eva hid her smile.

"She's almost not a little girl anymore," Adam said thoughtfully and with a little sadness. Eva saw that he realized that he was missing Diane's growing up, watching the subtle changes that for him were happening in yearly spurts and much too fast.

Adam began to absently stroke the back of Eva's neck. She found herself holding the plastic cup tightly in her hand while Adam's warm fingers sent waves of gentle delight down her spine.

"She's coming down to spend Christmas with me…so I won't be lonely," he finished, looking at her. Eva watched his wide mouth, his jaw. Her eyes came back to his. "You know what I'd like to do?" he questioned in a low deep voice.

"No...what?" Eva asked automatically, loving his rugged, uncompromising face, the strength and character edged around his eyes, and the earthy tobacco brown of his skin. Adam leaned a little toward her.

"I'd like to take you somewhere and make love to you again."

Eva caught her breath...felt a tightness in her chest. She'd thought that Adam had viewed last night as an inevitable episode. One that had satisfied his curiosity, even though she had acquiesced, and not necessarily to be repeated. Adam began to come closer as if to kiss her. But a soft, silky voice broke into their cocoon, and their surroundings came rushing back.

Adam and Eva turned their heads to find Lavona Morris standing indolently with her hands splayed seductively on her rounded hips. She called Adam's name again.

Eva pulled back from Adam feeling embarrassed and foolish under Lavona's derisive little smile. Eva looked at the cup in her hands. "I'm going to throw this away..."

"No! Stay here!" Adam's hand clamped down tightly on her arm. Eva looked at him and saw the hard set to his mouth. He didn't intend that she should bow away from Lavona's presence. But Eva didn't want to watch any exchange between Lavona and Adam, especially since last night.

Eva tried to stand up, but the large hand was firm and hard. She couldn't move. "Maxwell, please..."

"Dammit, Eva...don't argue with me!" Adam growled low. He watched her a moment longer and got up to walk over to Lavona.

A perverse curiosity had Eva turning to view the two. She couldn't help but notice what an outstanding couple they made, Adam with his tall, manly presence and La-

vona with her womanly charm. Their voices were low.
Lavona smiled up at Adam, moving her shoulders for
emphasis. Adam nodded and responded but stood with
his arms crossed, and, therefore, he was somewhat removed from Lavona. After only a few minutes Adam
turned away from her and back in the direction of Eva.
Lavona's face turned momentarily stormy. She sliced a
malevolent glare at Eva before the anger faded. Shrugging indifferently, Lavona turned and sashayed away.

Adam reached out for Eva's hand, and numbly she
placed hers into his. Only after he'd pulled her to her feet
and they were once again walking did she dare to look
at him. Maxwell was moving through the crowds, maneuvering them both and maintaining a firm hold of her
hand, as if he had no intention of letting her go.

"Maxwell?" Eva began when they'd left the square,
wanting to know what had happened. But he merely
looked down at her. A smile curved a corner of his
mouth.

"I'm taking you and Diane to dinner" was all he'd
say. But that's all that was needed. It would seem that
Adam had just made a choice and the choice was her.

Unbelievably Eva was filled with joy.

DINNER WAS a lighthearted affair at The Upper Deck, a
high hillside open-air restaurant overlooking St. John
with St. Thomas in the distance. Diane chattered away
happily, almost to herself, adjusted to the idea of going
home, knowing she'd be back again in six months. She
promised to write Eva and copied down the address on
the corner of a paper napkin.

Maxwell let the conversation flow basically around
him, only occasionally teasing with Diane in answering

a question from her. He and Eva exchanged looks and their communication was accomplished with their eyes.

It was dark when Adam pulled up behind Eva's Jeep, left in front of his house earlier in the day. Diane was worn out and sleepy as she climbed listlessly out of the vehicle.

"Have you finished packing?" Adam asked his daughter.

Diane yawned. "No, not yet. I'll finish in the morning…"

"You'll finish tonight," Adam corrected firmly. "You still don't remember where you last put your swimsuit."

"I'll find it," Diane whined petulantly.

"Now Diane…" Maxwell ordered very quietly. Diane cast him a cautious look, and gave in at once.

"Oh, all right…" was her soft reply.

"I won't see you tomorrow before you leave. Have a good trip home," Eva offered.

Diane sighed. "I wish you were flying back with me. You promise you'll write?"

Eva smiled. "I promise." Then she was completely taken by surprise when Diane almost threw herself against Eva, giving her a quick, thorough hug.

"I like you," Diane whispered, and then pulled away to run into the house.

Eva swallowed the rush of emotions welling up inside and turned away from Maxwell's penetrating gaze. Maxwell moved to stand close behind her.

"I'll come to see you later," he suggested. Eva shook her head and turned back to face him.

"No, don't do that. This is Diane's last night. You should spend it with her."

Maxwell scowled impatiently. "Look, I love Diane

very much, and I know I should stay here with her but...I want to make love to you, Eva!''

Eva grinned at him. ''Well, you'll just have to control yourself,'' she teased, nonetheless complimented. Adam cursed under his breath. He looked around him and, taking Eva's hand, pulled her around the side of the house. Against the side was a long but narrow chest. The top half was covered with a strip of black vinyl. Adam sat on it and, leaning back against the house, he pulled Eva onto his lap. Gathering her against his chest he proceeded to kiss her hungrily. Eva melted against him willingly, supported by his chest and arm around her back.

Adam's hand rubbed back and forth across her stomach to her side, turning her more into him. His mouth manipulated and pulled at hers, drawing a sweetness from her that made her weak and helpless in his hands. Under her bottom as she sat sideways on his lap, Eva could feel his arousal. She inadvertently wiggled to get more comfortable, and Adam shuddered and moaned into her mouth. His hand came back to her stomach and down to her leg. The hand stroked her partially bared thigh, but his hand could move just so far upward. Adam pulled his hand away.

''What the hell have you got on?'' he asked bewildered.

''It—it's a culotte,'' Eva whispered brokenly, suddenly in complete sympathy with his thwarted efforts. He cursed again and kissed her, grinding his mouth against hers savagely, pushing into the deep warm cavern of her mouth. But then he gentled his hold on her in an attempt to coax her to give in to him.

Adam located instead the hem of her lilac blouse and slipped his hand beneath. He moved against the smooth skin, locating and caressing one breast. Eva arched her back causing her taut nipple to push into the palm of his hand; her arms circled tighter around his neck.

Eva knew they had to stop right now. It was too close to the house and Diane. Eva truly didn't want Maxwell to leave his daughter. She twisted away and pulled out of his embrace. Standing up unsteadily, Eva could only hear their heavy breathing.

Adam stood up behind her. He gently put his arms around her and pulled her back against the length of him. Again Eva felt the hard outline of him. "Woman, you are cruel," he growled, kissing her ear and holding her to him.

"You'll survive," Eva whispered, not sure that she would. His hot breath and tongue tickled her earlobe.

"You sure I can't make you change your mind?" he asked in a thick voice, his hand roaming intimately over the curve of her buttocks. Eva moaned, turning her face against his chest.

"Ooooh, Max! You probably could," she admitted readily, "but I don't think you should."

Adam sighed and took a deep steadying breath of air. He turned her fully into his arms and his hands came up to cup her face. "You really don't want me to come to you?" he asked persuasively.

"I didn't say that. I—I just feel you should stay with Diane."

Her face was dark in the night, her forehead, nose, and cheeks highlighted by the moon. The eyes, however, were wide and bright, her mouth soft and full from his kisses. Adam moved his thumb over her lips.

"I can't be with you tomorrow, Eva. Or the day after that…"

She pulled away just a little from him. "I'm not asking

you to,'' she said tightly, inwardly disappointed nonetheless. ''You don't need to feel...''

''You don't understand...'' Adam cut her off, one hand circling her waist firmly to keep her still. ''I'm going down island with Lito tomorrow night. I'll probably be gone a week.''

The blood felt like it was draining from her face as she looked at him. How did he expect her to react? What did he expect her to say?

''Going fishing, I suppose?'' Eva attempted lightly. But Adam frowned at her flippant attitude. He dropped his hands, releasing her altogether.

''We left some experiments and traps along a hundred-mile route. It's time to go pull them in.''

''I see,'' Eva murmured, straightening her clothes. She began moving back to the front of the house and the Jeep. For just an instant she was tempted to say to Adam, *Yes, please come to me later. A week is too long to wait and see what will happen next.* But the thought was fleeting, and she kept silent on the subject. ''You better go in. Diane's going to wonder what happened to you.''

''She knows what happened to me...'' Adam remarked evenly.

Eva stopped and turned quickly back to face him, her eyes apprehensive. ''What?''

Adam put his hands on his hips and tilted his head to the side as he watched her face. ''Diane has informed me that it's okay with her if I want to kiss you.''

Eva's mouth dropped open. ''Di—Diane said that to you?''

''Uh-huh...'' he murmured. ''She said she understands that sometimes grown-ups have to be alone.''

''Oh my God!'' Eva groaned in shock. ''What must she be thinking of me?''

"She likes you, Eva. Much better than Lavona, obviously. She wasn't passing judgment on you." Adam stepped closer and frowned at her. "Are you embarrassed or ashamed of last night…or right now?" he asked softly.

She had been. But thought it unnecessary to say so. Especially now, knowing that she very much wanted to be with him again.

"I—I just don't want Diane to think about me the way she did Lavona."

Adam's jaw flexed. "Not hardly," he said.

Eva turned away and prepared to climb into her Jeep. Adam grabbed her wrist.

"What will you do the rest of the night?"

"Read. Wash my hair. And you?"

He chuckled soundlessly. "Help Diane get her things together…take a very long, very cold shower."

Eva smiled merrily up at him. Adam returned a slight smile as they looked at one another.

"I—I hope your experiments are okay," she said lamely.

"To hell with the experiments. What about me?" he asked, slowly trying to bring her back into his arms. Eva didn't resist. Her hands spread over his chest and Adam settled his hands on her lower back.

"You'll have Lito for company, and you'll be very busy. You don't expect me to believe you'll have time to think about me, do you?" she teased, but Adam didn't answer. He tightened his arms suddenly, forcing her harshly against his hips.

"Are you going into St. Thomas again?" Adam asked roughly. Eva puzzled over the question. Finally she shrugged.

"I don't know. I don't think so."

Adam seemed satisfied with the answer. "Since I have Diane's permission, can I kiss you goodnight?"

Eva laughed in real amusement. "Since when have you ever asked my permission for anything?"

"That's true…" he agreed huskily, and bent to quickly cover her mouth with his. The heat that had sparked between them before was evidently still burning. Adam forced her mouth open to probe inside, his hands running up and down her back. His mouth dragged to her cheek. "Maybe I should just ride with you to make sure you get home safely…" he groaned against her temple.

Eva pushed him away. "I'll go alone. I can take care of myself, remember?" She climbed into the Jeep and started the engine. Adam stood watching, his foot on the fender of his own vehicle, his hand resting on a muscled thigh.

"Kiss Diane for me." Eva shouted over the noise. "And I hope you have a good trip, too!" There was lots more she had on her mind to say. Like, be careful, and hurry back…and that she'd miss him. But she didn't. Eva wasn't going to be what Adam Maxwell expected her to be. So she kept all her real, deeper feelings inside and went home alone.

THE DINNER at Mildred Decker's was more welcomed than Eva had first anticipated. For one thing it didn't allow her to think about Adam Maxwell or to reminisce about their night together, which now was beginning to seem totally unreal to her. And for another, she missed him a great deal.

Eva wore a pair of white loosely draped summer slacks, and a black-and-white pin-striped camisole top. She brought along a rose-colored shawl in case the air was cold. Milly's house was a small unpretentious, charming structure on Chocolate Hole. It had a large flagstone entrance, the walkway continuing all around the house to a large open deck. The interior of the house was just one large, high-ceilinged room. The floor was done in pretty red Spanish ceramic tiles to offset the white stone walls and white decorations. The kitchen was along one wall, all the appliances and cabinets built together to save space. The living room/dining room occupied the rest of the space, with the living-room sofa opening up into Milly's bed at night. Eva mentioned that she thought the house an ideal design for one person. Milly laughed good-naturedly at the underlying suggestion.

"It discourages visiting relatives from the mainland. They know full well that if they come, they sleep in sleeping bags they bring with them!"

Eva laughed at Milly's ingenuity and honesty.

Milly's other guests, eight in all, proved to be a happy mixture of local friends and people transplanted from the mainland. There was one almost-elderly couple that ran chartered sailing from their boat. Anna Simpson was about forty and with the Virgin Islands Tourist Office. Margot Levine was there, as well as Richard Hollis, a transplanted Georgian who used to teach architecture, but now built houses. And the last guest was a distinguished-looking gentleman with soft gray hair and a beard, who was the manager of a local resort camp.

The evening was fun. Eva felt a little awed by the exciting professional lives these people led, but they all expressed great interest in the law firm she worked for and the kinds of chores she performed.

"You should just go ahead and try for a law degree," Anna encouraged. Eva smiled, remembering a comment Adam had made to her when they'd first met.

"It has been suggested," Eva admitted.

The dinner ran as late as Milly said it would. It was

well after midnight when everyone began to leave. Milly walked Eva to the door.

"Well, dear…I'm so glad you could come. I'm just sorry Maxwell couldn't make it, also."

Eva's head came up alert at the mention of his name. "Was he invited?"

"Oh yes," Milly said casually. "Once I knew you two had met, it made sense. You could have come together. But Adam said he'd be away. Did you know that?"

Eva nodded. "He told me he was going down island. But he never said he'd been invited to dinner."

Milly shrugged. "I'm not surprised. He is a pretty private person. But he did make me assure him that you'd get back to Hawksnest okay."

"Did he?" Eva asked, hard pressed to keep the surprise out of her voice.

"I told him there was no need to worry, of course. You aren't a bit like Lavona Morris. I suppose you know that they're an item?"

Eva cringed. "Yes…I—I'd heard."

"Well, Lavona can't do much of anything on her own but look pretty. Anything she's involved with usually requires the aid of a good-looking man. It's a pretty convincing helpless act."

Eva was acutely uncomfortable with the conversation, not believing that Adam was taken in by Lavona's act when she had so much else going for her. But she was also now uncertain herself that she meant anything more to Adam than Lavona did.

"I also told Adam you seemed pretty independent and capable to me…" Milly continued as she opened the door for Eva.

"What did he say to that?"

Milly laughed suddenly, shaking her head in memory. "Oh…he said something totally unrepeatable!"

Chapter Nine

It kept running through Eva's mind that Lavona Morris had said that Adam Maxwell wanted only one thing from her. Well, he'd gotten that. And there hadn't been much indication that there was to be anything more. If Lavona was also to be believed, Adam didn't want anything more.

There was no positive indication that Adam had given up Lavona in favor of her, but Eva knew that Adam was the kind of man who could have anyone, almost anytime he pleased. What if he was seeing them both?

These and other complicated scenarios continued to play out their dramas in Eva's mind the whole week Adam Maxwell was away. Eva alternately convinced herself she was a fool or that she was handling the situation well, from one day to the next. For one whole day she thought not of Adam at all. But then at night she tossed and turned, her nighttime fears and imaginings her own worst enemy. One day she sat on the beach watching every sailing vessel that anchored offshore, thinking each one was Adam returning early. And the next day she stayed away from the beach altogether. One moment she resolved to keep Adam at arm's length until she could safely get back on a plane headed for home. In the next moment she'd have feverish, breathless memories of her body reacting spontaneously and coming to life instinctively under his, of Adam's hands and mouth stroking and manipulating erotically in ways she never even dreamed of with Kevin.

Eva buried herself in reading, finishing five paperback books in four days. At night she crocheted, without a pattern or purpose, and the finished product was just something lacy, large, and round. She pulled a ribbon through the outer edges and made a drawstring purse. It was much too young for herself, so she lined it with a white linen handkerchief and mailed it to Diane.

She wrote a letter to her mother and was suddenly lonely. She got a postcard from Martin Isaacs, her boss, and wished his house could be hers forever.

She didn't go into St. Thomas again, but Deacon Butler did return once more to St. John. Eva was just stepping out of the pink postal building after mailing Diane's package. It was nine days since the beginning of Adam's trip, and her mind was temporarily free of him. Eva heard a lilting island voice behind her calling a welcome, which she ignored.

"Hey! Hey, beautiful lady. You not going to say hello?"

Eva never turned her head.

"Hey...Eva!" A rough hand grabbed her arm, and she turned to face the ever-smiling Deacon Butler. For an instant Eva had a vague image of a scowling, disapproving Adam Maxwell looming in the background. She smiled brightly at Deacon.

"Oh, hello! What are you doing here?"

He laughed, his ebony face wrapped in smiles.

"Don't you know, man? I come see you! You change

your mind yet about staying?'' Deacon asked without preamble.

"No, I haven't,'' Eva admitted ruefully.

"Then I have to try harder, yes?'' Deacon said, undaunted. He steered her toward the harbor, hooking Eva's arm around his own.

"How were you going to find me? What if I'd left already?'' Eva questioned in curiosity.

Deacon laughed. "Oh I know you still here. I ask my friends here. This is a small island…everybody know everybody.''

Eva groaned inwardly. As far as she was concerned, the island was getting smaller all the time.

They walked toward the attractive maze of shops and restaurants in Mongoose Junction and headed for the Moveable Feast, an airy, casual café with seating for brunch, lunch, and dinner, and with a square low bar in the middle of the room. Eva easily let herself be persuaded to have lunch with Deacon, feeling she needed an ego boost and a little easy company. They sat at a roomy square table and placed their orders.

"So…how you like Carnival, eh?'' Deacon asked, leaning across the table at Eva.

"Oh, it was fun! Everything was so colorful. I took lots of pictures.''

"Good…good.''

"Were you there? I didn't see you,'' Eva asked.

"No, I had to work that day. Anyway, everyone all the time say best Carnival on St. Thomas in the spring.''

"Well, I wasn't here in the spring, so for me this one was just great.''

Deacon smiled and nodded at her. Then his brows drew together in an uncharacteristic frown, even though his mouth continued to curve in a smile. He tilted his head to one side to look thoughtfully at Eva.

"How come a pretty lady like you is not married?"

Eva went still for a moment, her heart turning over with a flashing memory. She shifted in her chair and sat back against the comfortable canvas. "I—I was married," she finally said calmly, her fingernail tracing an old watermark from a glass on the black leather top of the table.

"What happen?" Deacon persisted. "You divorced… separated?"

Eva smiled vaguely at the only two possibilities Deacon recognized. "No…my husband is dead. He died in a house fire."

There was a curious pause, and Eva looked up at Deacon, at the sudden understanding and depth of sympathy in his eyes that he did not voice. She didn't wait for him to ask the next obvious question that was forming.

"We had a little girl. I lost her, too," she informed him quietly, a little surprised at how calmly she could now say it.

Deacon silently shook his head, his eyes lowered to the table. That was his total expression, and after that, he let the subject drop. He looked at her once again. "You like it here?"

"I love it here," Eva emphasized. "But I am going back home," she also added very clearly, so that her meaning could not be mistaken.

"When you coming back?" Deacon asked.

"I don't know…it depends," Eva answered with a shrug.

"On what?"

What indeed. Eva hadn't worked out a plan or details. It just depended. She must have had something in mind when she said that. She blinked rapidly and frowned at Deacon. "I—I don't know," she said honestly.

Deacon smiled at her, but this time the smile was more intimate…and warmer. Even his voice took on a rich, seductive quality, which alerted Eva and which stated what he was thinking in that moment.

"I like you very much, Eva. I'd be very happy if you stay here with Deacon."

Eva stared at him. She was flattered beyond words. But she found she couldn't answer him directly. She swallowed. "Deacon, there are lots of pretty available women here…" Eva thought of Anna Simpson, even of Lavona Morris. "How come you haven't married before?"

He laughed softly, sitting back in his chair as their plates were served.

"Oh. I'm very particular, you know. I been waiting for someone just like you!"

Eva shook her head sadly. "It—it can't be me, Deacon. I like you very much. You've helped to make my trip here really memorable, but…I can't stay here with you."

That effectively silenced them both for a time. Eva expected the lunch to then become a morbid affair. But it didn't. It was pleasant, enjoyable, and welcomed.

Afterward, Eva did not invite Deacon back to the house at Hawksnest, knowing it was useless and unnecessary to draw out the inevitable. Though they spent much of the afternoon walking through Cruz Bay, talking and laughing easily, when the five o'clock ferry left for St. Thomas, Deacon was on it. Eva knew she'd never see him again.

She became uneasy after that, restless. She had an anticlimactic feeling based on absolutely nothing. It was just there. She suddenly had a dread of going back to

Hawksnest and the house there. She suddenly didn't want to be alone, although she knew for certain she didn't want to be with Deacon Butler. Eva suddenly cursed the small tightness of St. John, which gave her a limited number of places to escape to. Sighing in frustration, Eva climbed into the Jeep and drove home feeling depressed.

Eva walked into the gallery and absently dropped her tote. She walked pensively into the kitchen and poured herself a glass of lemonade. She turned from the refrigerator with the glass almost to her lips. She noticed, then, a jacket thrown over her counter space. She looked down and saw a small black nylon duffle. Eva spun around and searched the gallery, finally locating Adam leaning against a column.

He had a full week's growth of beard, making him look positively rakish and very handsome. Eva's heart and stomach turned over at the sight of him, and unconsciously she broke into a bright smile.

"Maxwell!" she exclaimed, putting her untouched lemonade on the counter. Typically Adam didn't return a greeting to her. He was dressed in a pair of very faded jeans and a blue work shirt tucked into the waistband, but unbuttoned almost to the waist. The sleeves were rolled to the elbow. His skin color seemed even darker, if that was possible, from the intense sun on open waters.

Slowly Adam pushed himself from the pillar and moved toward her. His mouth was a hard straight line. Eva frowned in confusion at him, the smile fading from her lips.

"I've been waiting for you," he said low in a deceptively controlled tone.

"How long?" she asked, for want of anything else to say.

"Long enough," he responded shortly.

"What's that supposed to mean?"

"It means I thought you'd be here. You weren't on the beach. I saw Milly Decker, so you weren't with her. You didn't go into St. Thomas because the gate to the house entrance was unlocked..."

"I was in Cruz Bay having lunch," Eva said formally, tightening inside. Her gladness at seeing Adam was fast vanishing under his bombastic accusing tone of voice.

"Alone?" he asked scathingly.

Eva stood tall and crossed her arms over her chest. "What is this?" she asked defensively. Adam's jaw jerked in anger. "No, I wasn't alone. I was with a friend..." she said emphasizing the last word. Then she didn't wait for him to ask who. "It was Deacon Butler. You remember him. He's the cabdriver I picked up on St. Thomas. I think that's how you so nicely put it!" Eva didn't realize her voice was slowly rising in indignant anger. Adam suddenly reached and grabbed her by the upper arms, his fingers biting harshly into her skin. Eva gasped.

"I haven't even been home yet. Lito dropped me off here so I could see you. I thought you'd be here!" he ground out. Eva was bewildered at his attitude, and her own confusion and despondency had reached its peak. She jerked in his hold on her.

"Why should I have been? What right had you to expect me to be? I don't recall that you mentioned when you'd be back!"

"Perhaps I was wrong to expect a lot of things. Maybe I was right about you in the first place." Adam released Eva so abruptly that she went back against the counter, the edge hitting her back. "Telling me Deacon meant nothing to you, that you wouldn't see him again..."

"I never said any such thing! Deacon's a friend, Maxwell, and I like him as just that. And I didn't intend on seeing him again. He came to see me without any warning!''

''But you didn't send him away either!''

Eva's mouth dropped open. ''Why should I?''

''So you wouldn't lead the poor fool on as you did me.''

''As I did…. Get out!'' Eva screamed. ''Get out of here!'' She stamped her foot in frustration, her hands bunching into tight little fists.

Adam smiled unpleasantly at her. ''What's the matter? Did I hit on the truth?''

Eva arched a brow and laughed in derision. ''You wouldn't know the truth if it kicked you!'' She turned and picked up Maxwell's duffle. It was heavy, but her anger lent her strength, and she heaved and swung it toward him. The bag hit Adam in the chest, and his hands came up to grab and clutch it. His face contorted strangely and his brows drew sharply together. But then his face cleared. Eva never noticed in her mission to get Adam out of her sight.

''You have no rights over me! We don't belong to each other. And you have no right to pass judgment on me about whom I see!''

She threw his jacket at him. It also landed against his chest but slid lightly to the floor at his feet. Eva faced him, her hands on her slender hips, beside herself with outrage. When she thought of all those recent nights of not getting any decent sleep for thinking of him, she wanted to resort to physical violence.

''You have some nerve!'' Eva continued to rant. ''What have I ever said to you about Lavona? For all I know she was with you the whole week you were away! It's okay for you to do what you want, but I'm supposed to prove you wrong about me! Talk about double standards…''

"Okay, okay…you've made your point," Adam finally got in, his voice now oddly strained and shaky. "But for the record, Lavona wasn't with me…"

Eva laughed again. "Oh! And just because you say so I'm supposed to believe you?"

Adam leaned against a near pillar. Eva's anger had purged itself from her. Her chest was heaving in exhaustion, and she felt disappointed. She'd missed him so much, and for him now to treat her as if she was someone that he had a right to order about…tears began to fill her eyes and her vision blurred. Adam's images wavered and swam before her.

"This is silly…" Eva said in a choked voice, wiping her tears from her eyes and smearing them across her cheek. "Why are we yelling at each other? What difference does it make where I was? You don't think that much of me anyway." She sniffed and walked into the kitchen again, needing a tissue to blow her nose. Eva was feeling more depressed and dejected by the minute. After having located the tissue, she blew her nose and came back to face Adam again.

"I think you'd better go. I just want you to leave me alone." Her voice broke.

Adam's eyes were bleak as he stared at her. Eva couldn't begin to guess at what he was thinking. His head tilted backward as he took in a deep breath of air, his eyes closing momentarily, as if warily. "All right…I'll go," he acquiesced. There was no sarcasm, no more fight from him, and that immediately puzzled Eva.

Adam shifted the duffle to one hand and bent forward with a grunt to pick up his jacket. There was a fine mist of perspiration on his forehead, throat, and neck. He started walking toward Eva, heading for the door. Inside, Eva could feel herself relenting toward him.

"Did...did you have a good trip?" she found herself asking. Maxwell quirked a cynical brow at her.

"Do you really want to know?"

"Yes, I do," she informed him quietly. "I know those experiments were very important to you."

Adam looked at her thoughtfully, his eyes glazed and almost unfocused. Eva began to get suspicious and frowned at him. Adam nodded briefly. "It was a good trip..." Then he proceeded past her. Eva turned her head, still frowning, to look after him and gasped, bringing her hand to her mouth.

"Maxwell! You're bleeding!" she said in real shock, watching an ever-growing stain of dark red moisture spread along his side under his right arm.

But Adam never stopped, continuing through the entrance and unsteadily down the steps.

"Max!" Eva yelled frantically after him but he continued walking. Eva went after him. She grabbed his upper sleeve and jerked until his head turned in her direction. He looked at her, but Eva wasn't sure in that moment he was really seeing her. Adam seemed almost feverish to her.

"Oh, Maxwell..." Eva moaned in growing sympathy, her anger and earlier indignation completely forgotten. She was suddenly spurred into action. She took his duffle and threw it into the Jeep, followed by the jacket. "Get in!" Eva ordered Adam.

Adam wearily put his hands on his hips, seemingly unaware of his bloodied condition. "Look...I don't need..."

"What were you going to do? Go home and quietly bleed to death!" Eva said scathingly. Adam opened his mouth to speak. "Get in!" Eva said again. They stared at each other for long struggling moments, and then Maxwell slowly swung his tall frame into the passenger side of Eva's Jeep.

Eva ran back to the house for her tote and keys and returned seconds later to find Adam somewhat slouched in his seat, one foot braced on the opening, his arm hanging limply over his bent knee. Eva got in, got the Jeep into gear, and drove a little recklessly to Maxwell's house. The Jeep had barely come to a halt when Adam was struggling to get out, heading right for the door to unlock it and walk inside. He headed slowly for the bathroom. By the time Eva had followed him inside, Maxwell was returning to the living room with a hand filled with bottles, cotton gauze, tape, scissors, and a wet washcloth.

Eva turned on some lights and pulled out Maxwell's work stool for him to sit on. He began to pull the shirt from the jeans and, wincing once, shrugged the soiled shirt off his shoulders and down his arms. Eva caught it before it hit the floor and took it to the kitchen to run water on it before the blood stains set.

The thick gauze padding already taped to Maxwell's side was soaked through with blood, and he contorted his body trying to lift the material away. It stuck to the wound.

"I'll do it..." Eva said, gently pushing his hands away. Her own hands began to shake as she gingerly removed the gauze from the torn, tender flesh, causing Maxwell to stiffen in pain despite his silence. "What happened?" Eva's voice croaked when she saw the raw open wound.

"Easy," Adam said in a low voice. "It's not as bad as it looks."

"But what happened?" Eva took the washcloth and

began dabbing around the wound, soaking up the blood. It was not a large gash, but it did seem to be deep.

"A steel securing line snapped onboard ship…" He winced.

"I'm sorry!"

"It whipped into my side, and it had sharp teeth!" Adam quipped, but Eva saw his jaw clenching and unclenching in pain, and his brow was damp with perspiration.

"Maxwell, why didn't you have Lito do something!"

"He didn't see how deep it was…and I just wanted to get back to St. John…" Eva looked up into Adam's heavy-lidded eyes and saw his full meaning in the look he gave her.

"You—you should have stitches," she said vaguely, more intent on the look in his light eyes.

"No…it's not that bad. And it will heal better open…"

Eva suddenly remembered the way her mother had handled serious cuts and gashes and went about making sure Adam's wound would not get infected. Then she taped fresh gauze on the wound, as tight as she could make it. Adam let out a long tight sigh when she was finished. Eva looked anxiously at him, realizing that he had been in a lot of pain and was now exhausted.

"I think you should go to bed," Eva said calmly.

"Is that a suggestion…or an offer?" Adam asked, but winced again in pain as he stood up. He bent his head and put his hands on his waist to steady himself. "Never mind," he groaned. "I couldn't do a damned thing anyway."

Moving slowly and tiredly, he got to his room. Eva followed, returning all the medication to the bathroom. When she peeked into Adam's room, the light was off, and he had his sneakers off and was just pulling down his jeans. Eva tried to ignore his stepping out of his shorts as she pulled back the light bedspread and held it up as he climbed onto the bed.

Adam sprawled in complete collapse as Eva brought the spread only up to his waist. He was asleep before she left the room. Eva hugged herself and walked slowly back to the living room. She felt as if she'd just been swept through the center of a wind storm with it pulling and tearing at her, leaving her breathless, confused, and excited.

She'd had more varying emotions wash over her in a period of an hour than she'd had in a whole year. That it should all begin and end in one person as abrasive as Adam Maxwell also left her scared. She'd never had such strong feelings for anyone but Kevin. But Kevin was gone, and Maxwell was here…and she was here with him.

It had upset her greatly the way he'd attacked her. But she was too exhausted herself and concerned about him to give much thought or analysis to his ridiculous accusations.

Eva sat in a chair thinking about the man and wondering at a number of conflicting feelings she had for him, not the least of which were both anger and concern. Her first sight of him leaning against the pillar had also sharply defined the extent that she'd missed him. That had been scary, too. And then his rugged appeal had instantly reached deep within her and began to stir desire in her, warm and flowing.

After a long time Eva brought in his things from the Jeep. And she made herself coffee. Later still she looked into Adam's darkened room to find him breathing deeply, the sleep of someone beyond instant call. He hadn't shifted positions and, in fact, didn't move or make a sound for the next sixteen straight hours.

At eight the next morning, Eva slipped away to drive back to her own house, to shower and change clothes. She'd only napped off and on all night, but it just wasn't in her to leave him all alone. She changed into a black short-sleeved T-shirt and white cotton pants with an elasticized waist. She brushed her hair into its adopted summer style and drove back to Maxwell's. He was still asleep.

Eva made herself busy trying to get the blood out of Adam's shirt. Thinking he might have specimens in his duffle, she emptied it, but only found dirty clothes. She washed those, too. At noon, her stomach protested angrily her lack of attention to it, and she made some boiled eggs and toast, taking it up to the roof deck to sit in the sun. But the sun made her sleepy, and after an hour or so, she came back down.

She checked on Adam again and found him turned on his stomach, one leg drawn up almost to his chest. The cover was almost down to his knees, giving Eva a look at his smooth brown back. She came just close enough to see the bandaged wound had not bled again and, pulling the covers up once more, she went back to sit in a chair.

Eva wasn't sure what time she fell asleep. And she certainly had no idea what time it was that Adam finally woke up and came naked to the living room and found her curled up in a chair, a magazine sliding off her lap to the floor. She felt herself being gently lifted and her head rolling in a fog onto a smooth hard plane. She never really felt the need to move and come fully awake, because she felt perfectly safe where she was. Then she was being lowered and stretched out on a flat, warm surface.

Eva felt hands pulling at her T-shirt, bringing it up and over her head. She frowned, shaking her head, the sudden air tautening the brown peaks of her small breasts. Her arms came up to cover herself. Her eyes blinked open once in the already dark room.

"No…" she whispered.

She was pulled against another hard surface, this one with a soft curly center.

"No, Maxwell…" Eva moaned, blinking again and finding Adam leaning over her, his bearded face very close. "You can't. Your side…" she whispered.

"I want to," Adam whispered back, pulling her arms down from her chest. He moved his head from her line of vision, and Eva next felt his warm moist mouth close firmly over a breast. She moaned, twisting her head.

"Max…stop…"

"Do you want me to stop?" he asked softly, a hint of hoarseness in his voice.

"Oh, no—no! But your side…"

"Then be quiet," he growled gently into her neck, but the words had no harshness to them…only impatience. His large hand slipped under the elastic of her pants and pulled both outer and under garments down together, over her feet, and dropped them to the floor. His hand came to spread flat on her stomach. Eva quivered under the warm hand.

"Max?"

"What?" he asked, his mouth now finding the other breast. Eva arched herself closer to the source of such exquisite pleasure.

"I—I've never kissed anyone with a beard before…"

Surprisingly, Adam chuckled. "There's a first time for everything."

"I thought it would scratch," Eva ventured in a raspy whisper as he continued to stroke her. Adam lifted his head to see her pretty brown face.

"Does it?" he asked thickly.

Eva put her arms around his neck and drew his head down to her. "It tickles…" she said with a smile. Adam kissed her with exploratory gentleness for a long time, feeling her return kisses beginning to match his in ardor and intensity. He moved finally to lie over her, to separate her knees, but, suddenly he went stiff with pain as his body stretched. Adam fell backward, his arms around Eva bringing her on top of him.

Eva suddenly felt a certain sense of exotic illicitness about what she was doing. Adam's hand on her hips shifted her position.

"Max?" Eva questioned as he settled her over his hips. "I can't, Max…I—I've never…"

"I'll show you," he crooned in a seductive voice. His hands cupped her bottom and he rotated his hips. Eva gasped, bracing her hands on his chest as the position began to have its effect.

"Oh!" Eva moaned in surprise. Adam gave a lusty guttural laugh, deep in his throat.

If Adam was feeling any ill effects or weakness from his accident, it was never made known to Eva. And at least for the next day and a half together in the house, neither cared.

EVA STOOD in front of the mirror gnawing at her bottom lip. She twisted the fabric and pulled and smoothed and wasn't sure this was a good idea. Her face was deep in concentration as she tried to see the blue java wrap from all angles. It was very pretty fabric, but was the garment decent? There was only one other piece of clothing on her besides the wrapped cloth, and Eva felt very undressed!

Sighing in exasperation Eva turned away from the mirror and stepped into high-heeled open-toed clogs. She then located her rose shawl, grabbed a straw clutch, and went into the living room. Her watch showed she still had fifteen minutes, but experience had already taught her that Maxwell hated to be kept waiting.

Eva still felt stunned and surprised at his declaration that they would have dinner at the exclusive restaurant at Caneel Bay Plantation, a resort on St. John. Adam hadn't asked her, as was also his habit; he simply told her it would be. And there hadn't been any question on Eva's part that she would agree.

Eva stayed with him nearly three days before a belated sense of caution drove her back to her own dwelling. Adam had not been pleased about that, and they'd argued. But then they spent a long time making up on the warm surface of the roof deck before they finally parted, both satiated and much more peaceful.

Adam's wound healed rapidly with Eva giving it much more care and attention than Adam himself, who only seemed to tolerate her fussings over the open injury. It also seemed a foregone conclusion that they'd spend their time together, much of it making love. Eva's previous lack of experience vanished with the developing days. She had a reminder, however, one morning that she was playing a dangerous game, and she set about taking personal precautions before her luck ran out.

She was amazed at the change in herself. She had finally left completely the mire of her tragedy, though Kevin and Gail in some special ways would be with her

all the days of her life. But she discovered again that life
was for the living.

And so she did.

When Adam arrived to get her, he stood a moment
with obvious admiration in his eyes that made Eva's heart
race. He had finally shaved off the beard, and when his
eyes had finished their appraisal and approval of her, his
grin turned into a tender half smile, the very first he'd
ever given her. Eva was stopped cold by the handsome
change in his features, a deep dimple slashed in a curve
of one cheek.

"Is that going to stay up?" Adam asked caustically,
referring to Eva's java wrap.

"I hope so," Eva commented wryly.

"So do I. I'm looking forward to a long, leisurely
meal…"

"With no interruptions?" Eva supplied.

Adam looked at her, quirking a brow and tilting his
head thoughtfully. "I may not mind a surprise or two.
We'll see…"

The restaurant was glorious, facing on the bay toward
the twinkling distant lights of St. Thomas. The tables
were large and beautifully laid out with flowers, wine
glasses, and candles. Eva had no idea to what she owed
this fairy-tale evening, but spending it with Maxwell
added to the beautiful fantasy.

They started with a chilled strawberry soup, followed
by an island salad with avocado and conch. There was a
basket of warm breads with soft sweet butter. Adam had
stuffed veal chops and Eva the fish, grouper prepared
with a cream and mushroom sauce. Neither had dessert,
electing instead to have liqueurs in the lounge while listening to the soothing tunes of a local calypso band.

They leisurely walked the grounds of the beautiful resort, well lit in the dark, all the way to Paradise Beach, where, taking off their shoes, they walked in the sand.

"It's a lovely night," Eva sighed. "Look at all the stars! You can never see them so bright back home."

"Do you know the stars?" Adam asked in his deep voice, standing behind her. He had an arm around her waist and stomach, holding her to him.

"No. Not at all…" Eva shook her head.

"Lito showed me how to find my way by them." Adam dropped his shoes in the sand and pointed with his free hand. "You see those three bright stars?" He pointed to form a triangle.

"Yes, I see them."

"Well, that forms the Summer Triangle. There's Denab, Vega and Altair. Each of those stars is in a different constellation. Now if you look just to the right, you'll see Hercules. There are five stars…"

Eva was laughing softly. "Maxwell, it's hopeless. I'll never see what you see."

Adam turned her to face him and looked down into her upturned face. "It doesn't matter," he said smiling at her. "When I teach you to sail…"

"Teach me to sail!" she said incredulously.

"It's simple."

"But I don't need to know."

Adam took her shoes from her hands and dropped them as well. "You can never tell," he crooned.

His hands made to wind around her waist further, but his fingers were caught in the gently gathered folds of the java wrap. Adam pulled his hands free but the fabric loosened around Eva, and she gasped, grabbing for it. Adam's rich bass laughter rang through the night. He began to pull the cloth.

"Maxwell! What do you think you're doing!" Eva asked scandalized.

"This is large enough for us both to lie on!"

A tug of war began to take place, Eva struggling to keep the fabric around her otherwise naked body.

"Stop it!" she hissed. But Adam was hugely entertained. When she continued to pull, he reached out a hand and began to tickle her. The results were instantaneous, and Adam stood holding the fabric completely within his grasp.

"I'll never forgive you for this!" Eva whispered, but she couldn't keep the laughter out of her voice. Maxwell's laughter continued to ring out.

"If you're nice to me, I'll give it back."

"Max! Please! Someone might see me!" she said making a grab for the cloth. It was jerked away.

"Be nice…" he reminded her.

Eva replied, "You're mean!" Her arms crossed her chest. Then she walked in front of Adam. Placing her hands on his chest, she reached up to kiss his mouth.

"Please, Max…" she begged.

Adam put a hand to the back of her head and held her still while he kissed her again more thoroughly. Then slowly he draped the fabric around her. Eva caught the ends and hastily twisted them to secure the garment once more. She was barely finished before Adam had her back in his arms.

"From now on I'm wearing real clothes!" Eva declared in exasperation.

"Don't do it on my account," Adam murmured, nuzzling her neck and ear.

"You have no appreciation for the trouble I went through. It's difficult wearing this!"

Adam worked his way up to her chin with his mouth. "It is clever," he admitted. "And very convenient," he added finally reaching her mouth, and his hands found her bare flesh again under the folds of the wrap.

Chapter Ten

Eva lay stretched out on her stomach, her head resting on her folded hands. The ship pitched from side to side with the gentlest movement and, with her eyes closed, it was soothing and comforting. She had positioned herself in the narrow shadow created by the main sail, avoiding the intense scorching sun as it beat down upon the open water and the lone ship temporarily anchored. It was so quiet and still that she could have been the only person left in the world. Except for Maxwell. But he was somewhere under the ship, deep below the aqua surface of the sea.

Eva's eyes cracked open just enough to make out the lines of the horizon beyond the bow of the ship. It was very easy to see how someone once believed that the world was flat and that you could just fall off the edge if you went far enough. But Eva also realized that beyond that calm, flat edge, somewhere north, was home. Soon she'd have to leave St. John and go back there.

Not once in all the time since she'd first met Adam Maxwell was any mention ever made of that inevitable date. He knew she was on vacation, but he treated it as indefinite, beginning perhaps when they first came together as lovers and continuing apparently without any end. But Eva knew better. Often in the last two weeks she wished she didn't. She wanted this idyll to go on and on. Common sense told her otherwise.

It had been a singularly startling moment when she fully realized that it was entirely possible for her to love another man in her lifetime other than Kevin Duncan. It had been heart-stopping to recognize that that man could be Adam Maxwell. Suddenly Eva saw Adam in a new light that rounded him out as a whole person in her mind. He could be arrogant and aloof, sarcastic and hard. But he also had a sense of humor. He had a quick temper, but he could be incredibly gentle. He had strengths and weaknesses. He was lusty and loving, and Eva found that she could deal with all of that in the man, and that it all endeared him to her.

Yet, what did it mean? And what did it matter? She had to go home. She'd been happy here in the Caribbean, but she didn't belong here. She had to go back to her own life. Maxwell would continue here, poking around seaweed and wiggly sea creatures, sailing a small ship expertly on the open sea, having his daughter grow up and out of his life, and managing nicely without Eva.

Eva's mind had also latched on tenaciously to a comment that Lavona Morris had made. Maxwell didn't want anyone permanent in his life and didn't need anyone permanent. He could, perhaps better than most, do exactly what he wanted with his life, breezing in and out of short-term affairs, never responsible for anyone but himself. From what she'd learned of Maxwell, Eva knew that this course of action was entirely possible for him. He was capable of being alone. He had learned to be alone. Well, so had she, and she had to go back to that singular life she'd adapted to, with the loving support of her mother, brothers, nieces and nephews to see her through. But she now found the prospect gnawing at her in an unsettling and unhappy way.

There were sounds from the water and things thudding in the bottom of the launch, tied to the side of the ship. There followed the shortest silence until Maxwell's huge, wet, glistening body sprang over the side and onto the wooden deck.

Through the small opening of her lazy eyes, Eva watched his well-sculptured body flex, watched his deep-chested breathing from his physical exertions, watched the muscular columns of his legs as they braced apart for balance against the swaying vessel.

Adam leaned over the side again and hauled up a bucket on the end of a twined rope and carefully sat his specimens down. His head turned to see her lying in repose, and Eva thought she saw the smallest smile curve his mouth. Thinking she was asleep, Adam walked carefully over to her. He held his arms out over her and began shaking them vigorously, sprinkling Eva with cold salty water.

Eva gasped. "Max!" she cried, wincing away from the water and coming to a sitting position as she pushed him away. Adam chuckled and turned back to the waiting bucket of specimens.

Eva drew her knees up to her chest and clasped her arms around them. She was wearing the bright tangerine swimsuit today, and it set off the rich brown of her skin, darkened even more now in the tropic sun, to perfection. Eva smiled at the reasoning that she'd worn the suit in self-defense. The black halter suit had too convenient a closing for Maxwell's quick hands, and he'd grown very adept at getting it off her quickly. Physically he was not to be denied, but she knew in all honesty that she'd long ago given up raising feeble objections. Eva enjoyed having Adam make love to her.

"Do you want help?" she asked from her shaded hovel.

Adam looked at her. "You don't have to. I know some of this turns you off."

Eva grinned, already beginning to move toward him. "I'm brave. I can take it," she teased.

Adam had to tell her very little. She'd helped him before, and the common sense routine had stayed with her. They worked quickly and efficiently in silence.

During the past weeks Adam sometimes had to go off on his own for a day, sometimes two. He would just announce he was going, and Eva would simply wish him a good trip. Sometimes she'd plan her own day without him, visiting ruins, lunching with Milly Decker, sitting quietly on the open gallery reading or down on the beach writing postcards and letters. Adam seemed to take these separations in the same light as she did, as an indication that they were separate people who perhaps at times needed to be alone and apart. It made the times together a special joy.

But Eva also knew that the arrangement lent them both some control. For Adam, perhaps that he was indeed master of his own ship. And for Eva, ever aware of Adam's earlier accusations about her, that she would not prove him right in those accusations. Therefore, she was really herself and not like everyone else he'd ever known.

They finished putting the jars into coolers, and Eva dug out some lunch for them. Adam almost never ate anything if he was snorkeling or diving for samples. But Eva sat and watched him in amazement as he drank nearly half a gallon of cold orange juice.

Adam sat on the deck surface, his back against the side

of the boat. Eva sat a little away from him, her legs folded gracefully to her side. She was restopping the thermos of juice and not immediately aware of the thoughtful deep look Adam was giving her. Eva suddenly looked up and caught his eyes, the light of his seemed eerily lighter in the brown of his face. Sitting in the afternoon sun was causing his body to sweat, and his broad chest was beaded with moisture under the dark curly hair, as were his shoulders and arms.

"Come here," he ordered low to her. A message of desire was already beginning to vibrate between the two of them.

"I'll think about it." Eva smiled saucily, not moving.

Adam grunted. "If I have to come and get you, you'll be sorry," he threatened.

Their eyes held.

"Brute!" Eva responded easily. But then very slowly, taking her own sweet time, she uncurled herself and stood up. She picked up a towel and walked toward the seated Adam.

Eva knelt down beside his outstretched legs and raising her hands to his chest, began to slowly and gently wipe away the moisture. Adam sat still through her ministrations, still searching over her face, his eyes exploring every detail. Eva meantime was methodical and slow in her task, ending by wiping the perspiration from Adam's forehead and chin.

Adam's hands took hold of her waist, turned her, and pulled her down to sit on the deck next to him. Eva's slender legs stretched out next to his, but he turned her shoulders so that her back was against his chest, and he put a long arm around her waist to hold her to him.

Eva sighed inwardly, wondering if Adam felt as much contentment and peace as she did. They often sat quietly for long periods of time without conversation. Adam was a private man, keeping much of his thoughts and feelings inside. They did, however, talk often about his work or Diane. But there were still things she did not know or understand about him. And he often chose the oddest moments to impart information to her. Like now.

Adam chuckled low, suddenly. The sound was a deep thud against his chest wall. "My wife was a lousy sailor..." he murmured vaguely. He stroked his hand across her latex-covered stomach. Eva quivered both from the sensual gentleness of the motion and the opening of Adam's conversation.

"I bet you'd never been on a boat in your life before coming here," he stated rather than asked.

"That's true," Eva agreed softly, her heart beginning to race for a still-unknown reason. There was a pause as Adam let his head go back to rest on the hard low railing of the ship.

"I was working on a research fellowship when I first met her. She was really fine. I couldn't figure out why the hell she was in an advanced biology course. Not with her looks!"

"Don't be chauvinistic," Eva murmured without thinking.

"Yeah...that's what she said, too!" Adam added caustically. He slid his hand back to its beginning resting point on her stomach. "She was a sophomore...and she really knew what she was doing. She was very good in biology," he said with a note of renewed surprise.

Eva began to be very uncomfortable with the talk. They'd never spoken about his ex-wife. As a matter of fact, he'd made it very clear once he didn't want to discuss her.

"Max…" Eva began, uncertain as to where this was heading now.

"Shhhh!" he said. His hand stroked again and tightened its hold imperceptibly to keep her still. "We got together…I mean, we really hooked up," he stated. "We were going to be this dynamic duo. The first black husband-and-wife research team in marine sciences. She kept better notes and records. I did better research. She finished school, and I got a civilian job with the Navy. And we got married…"

There was a long pause again and a muscle tightened in Maxwell's arm and leg. Eva could feel his whole body tighten up. Even his voice changed now with the previously unspoken-of memory.

"The very first time we ever got on a boat for a weekend fishing trip to test out a theory, she got sick. She was sick the whole three days. Then she decided she hated the sight of fish…and the smell, and the sea…and boats!" Maxwell laughed harshly, without humor. "That wiped out everything."

Maxwell turned his head just enough to rest the side of his jaw and mouth against her hairline and temple. His voice changed again…softened, if that was possible for him. "You've never gotten sick. I bet the thought never entered your mind."

He was wrong on the last count, but Eva didn't say so. She was feeling a welling of tears behind her eyelids. Suddenly she didn't want to know about his wife. She didn't care. And she certainly didn't want to be compared to her.

"And then it was my turn…" Adam was continuing. "Research wasn't a real job, she said. It was glorified busywork. She wanted more security, a home…kids, more attention. So I gave her a home, and we had Diane. That helped for a while."

He let out a sigh, some kind of long-standing tension dissolving in him and flowing outward. "Never have a kid because you think it will help," Adam said firmly.

Eva fought the tears. No, she wouldn't…ever. She and Kevin had Gail because they desperately wanted a baby. A baby seemed a natural extension of themselves.

"Was—was she angry at you for not giving up research?" Eva asked in a quiet, strained voice.

"I don't know." Maxwell shrugged. "We were angry at each other. It seems so crazy now that the whole thing happened. I thought it was exciting finding someone who knew what I was all about. But she had other plans for me…and herself. She tried to make me something I wasn't. I thought she was something she wasn't. Who knows."

Eva could see what a costly emotional mistake it had been for both of them. Maxwell was leery. He was never going to make that kind of mistake again. It was easier this way, being alone, not needing anyone. That's what he was trying to tell her. Don't expect anything. Don't ask for anything. He'd finally gotten his life worked out and he didn't want changes. Changes make you different.

Eva twisted in Maxwell's arms and reached up to press her lips to his. She was almost shaking, and her breathing was erratic. She'd taken Adam completely by surprise. He sat stunned for a moment by her sudden overture. But he quickly recovered. His arms closed around her, pulling Eva onto his lap, his mouth opening to really kiss her deeply. Eva kissed him with an abandoned fervor that surprised them both.

She'd already decided she'd ask nothing of him. And right now she only wanted to give, and that was made very clear to Adam. He groaned. He held her and shifted, swinging her down until her back was against the hard damp deck. Adam's tongue furrowed deep inside her mouth, knowing its contours very well. His hands pulled the thin straps to her suit down her arms, until her breasts were exposed with their sun-warmed centers. Eva's chest rose and fell rapidly.

Adam looked at her, frowning slightly, perhaps wondering at her urgency. Then he bent to kiss her more gently as she held back nothing from him. Tears rolled from her closed eyes, down her cheeks into her hairline. He quickly removed the last barriers between them and, settling himself with a moan, he brought them together.

The sun was unbelievable on his naked back. His skin was burning hot under her hands. But Maxwell never noticed, and after a short time she didn't either.

They were moving together in space. Higher and higher into the sky, into cool wind-swept air, into dark-blue star fields twinkling behind her eyelids madly, almost blinding her with their light. Speeding through time until it completely stripped her lungs of air, as Maxwell held and rode with her. There was a rhythmic cadence to their movement, Maxwell the stronger of the two and leading the way. His thrusting made it all go faster until Eva was dizzy and breathless, aching and exhilarated by his demands. She couldn't let go, afraid she would crash alone.

But then the speed was too fantastic, and they had to come back. It washed through her, making her cry out his name with the sudden reversal in feeling. She clung to Maxwell's damp body, silently begging him not to let anything happen to her. And he was careful. Slowly, gently, caressingly, bringing them both back to earth. Delightfully exhausted but safe. Eva's heart raced, and so did his. And she clung to Adam even more.

She changed her mind. It was no longer a question of being able to love him. And maybe it hadn't been for longer than she knew. She did love him. She loved Adam Maxwell beyond imagination... But she was going home. She had to. Soon...sooner.

Tomorrow if she could.

EVA USED HER HIP to push the door closed, and she immediately began to riffle through the mail on the foyer table. All bills and advertisements. She sighed, putting them back without interest, and left her leather work folio leaning against the table leg on the floor. Without admitting it to herself, it was the prospect of hearing from Maxwell that gave her the impetus to check the mail every day.

She heard low voices in the living-room and wondered which one of her mother's friends was visiting so close to suppertime. Eva bypassed the living room entrance and went into the kitchen. Something awfully good was roasting in the oven, and rice was simmering in a saucepan on top of the stove.

Carrots in the process of being sliced lay on the counter with a discarded paring knife. Eva frowned at the apparent interruption that had taken her mother from the kitchen. It was unlike her not to finish what she was doing, even when gossiping with neighbors.

Eva picked up half a raw carrot and stuck it in her mouth. She dropped her shoulder bag on a kitchen chair and peeled off the jacket to her lightweight navy-blue summer suit and put it on top of the bag. She bit into the hard crunchiness of the carrot and walked from the kitchen through the dining room, already beginning to talk.

"Mom, if you're busy, I can finish the…"

Inside the living room Eva stopped dead in her tracks, her heart skipping a beat painfully. Florence Stewart sat in a highbacked chair, her head with its short, iron gray hair bending around the chair to watch the approach of her daughter. But Eva's eyes were riveted wide open to Adam Maxwell standing in the middle of the room, dwarfing everything around him. He stared back at her evenly, but Eva knew at once the underlying anger that burned through his eyes and from his tightly clenched jaw.

Eva gulped down the mouthful of carrot and moved reluctantly into the room. Her mother was saying something to her, but she never heard a word. Maxwell held her mesmerized. He was dressed in a short-sleeved white shirt with a dark brown tie. His trousers were a khaki color and expertly cut and fitted to his physique. He seemed the epitome of masculinity to Eva in that instant. And he had lost none of his appeal for her.

Blood felt like it was draining from her head, and she felt momentarily giddy. Her ears were ringing, and her mother stood and mouthed meaningless, soundless phrases to her. Then Florence Stewart gave up. She clicked her teeth, shaking her head, and threw up her arms in resignation. Walking past her temporarily paralyzed daughter, she pulled the carrot remains out of Eva's hands and went back to her kitchen.

Maxwell braced his hands on his hips, more than likely from want of anywhere else to put them. He and Eva stared at one another.

"Hello, Adam," Eva whispered.

Maxwell scowled disagreeably at her. "You never called me Adam."

"It is your name," Eva reminded him lightly.

"That's not what I mean!" He arched a brow at her. Slowly his eyes swept the length of her, making particular note of the front slit of a modest depth in the front of her slim navy skirt, also noting the high-heeled beige pumps and the soft rose color of her boat-neck silk blouse. Her hair was softly curled and layered.

"You look different," he observed caustically. Then there was a pause.

"How?" Eva tilted her head slightly to the side.

Maxwell barely shrugged. "You look…efficient. Professional…very sophisticated."

Eva grimaced with a small smile. "It's mostly show…"

"I'm not used to seeing you with so many clothes on," he continued with a show of impatience.

Eva's brows shot up, and Maxwell, not ever given to embarrassment, shifted uncomfortably as his meaning sank in and registered. "The setting is different now. I can't wear a bathing suit and cover-up to work. I do work, you know," Eva also reminded him. Maxwell didn't respond to that.

Eva locked her fingers together in front of her, a little more settled now that the initial shock had worn off. She felt a certain breathless excitement at actually finding him in her living room and with the recognition that for whatever reason Adam Maxwell had come to find her. And even as he stood angry and cold in front of her, she knew she'd missed him very much, almost to the point of pain. Eva tilted her head further and pursed her lips thoughtfully.

"You look different, too," she said. Maxwell rocked a little on his feet and crossed his arms over his chest challengingly. "Mostly very uncomfortable."

"I am," Adam admitted. "I can't remember the last time I wore a tie!"

Eva smiled a bit more openly at his remark because it was said without any conscious attempt at humor.

"Then you've really made quite a concession."

"Thank you," he said sarcastically.

"I think I like it," Eva murmured flippantly. "It makes you look..." She searched for the word.

"Real?" Maxwell supplied, raising his brows.

Eva cringed inwardly. That had always been obvious to her. He was more real to her now than ever. "I was going to say, distinguished," she said softly.

Silence fell between them again. Eva imagined that something like pain flickered through Adam's eyes. But it was gone very quickly as they faced each other.

"Why did you just leave like that, without saying anything?" Adam finally asked angrily. His tone surprised Eva. She turned from him and walked to the other side of the room, not immediately answering.

It wasn't as if she hadn't thought of telling him. But having realized her deep feelings for him, she was actually afraid he'd do something like merely wish her a safe trip back home. Or even worse, say that it had been fun. She'd already been through the fantasies of his returning to Lavona's arms, if she'd have him back. But somehow Eva didn't think there'd be any question of that.

"We were together one afternoon, and I told you I had to fly to St. Croix for two days. I come back and you're gone!" he fairly exploded at her. Then he moved to stand in front of her, not letting her escape the confrontation.

"You must have known that I would come home eventually," Eva reasoned, not looking at him. "After all it was only a vacation."

"Quite honestly, I hadn't thought of it. I was busy with

other things at the time!'' Adam said caustically. ''I agree I was pretty stupid to think our time together meant anything to you!''

''That's not true! It—it was very special,'' Eva defended, looking now with appeal into his tightly drawn face.

''Then how could you just leave?'' Adam stormed at her, an angry cord in his neck bulging prominently.

''I—I didn't want to put you on the spot.''

Adam frowned, his eyes searching hers. ''What are you talking about?'' he asked in a deep, confused voice. Eva lowered her eyes to the subtle embroidery of his brown-on-brown tie. She hugged her arms around her waist.

''I didn't want you to feel obligated or pressured or sorry for me. I didn't want you to do or say anything then that you wouldn't have otherwise.''

Adam's expression became bleak and cold. ''So you made the decision for me. You didn't give me much credit, did you? Was I that insensitive? Did you trust me so little with your feelings and pride that you had to—to just sneak away?'' He gestured vaguely in the air with a hand. Eva looked into his rugged face.

''Max…it was never my feelings I was worried about…but yours!'' Eva was surprised that he hadn't figured that out. But Maxwell looked at her blankly, truly lost as to her meaning. In that instant, she actually smiled. The amazing Adam Maxwell did not know everything after all.

Eva's voice grew soft and gentle as she tried to explain. ''It was you who said I was like every other woman. It was you who told me what it was I really wanted and how I really am. You, Maxwell! And if you ever saw or learned anything differently you never said so."

As she talked, Maxwell watched her face with a thoughtful frown. In the background Eva heard a pot top being put into place on a saucepan. Probably the carrots, she thought, with complete irrelevance to the moment. And then the yard door from the kitchen opened and closed.

"Perhaps I did learn something, Eva," Maxwell admitted. "But maybe it's all too late," he added with a kind of finality that was not only sad but lonely...and sorry as well.

How could she tell him it was never too late. But then she had no idea why he was really here before her now. Was it just out of anger and hurt pride? Or was it something more significant? "What did you learn?" Eva asked him softly, as if the gentleness of her voice would coax the truth out of him.

He came several steps closer to her, pushing his large hands into his trouser pockets. "I learned that you know how to take care of yourself. You are a lot stronger than I ever thought you'd be." He moved his eyes slowly, searchingly, over her features. "And you probably don't need anyone. You don't need me."

Eva couldn't stand it. She couldn't bear to see him so uncertain and struggling with feelings that were hard for him to admit to, truths that were hard to believe.

Adam shook his head. "You deserve romance. You should have gentleness. I'm not any of those things. But I wish I could give them to you."

Eva's heart turned over at his admission. Maxwell walked past her to the window overlooking the back of the house and a screened-in sun porch. Eva reached out a hand to touch him, but drew it back.

In the yard Adam saw Eva's mother, an attractive, plump woman in her mid-sixties, as she hung up freshly washed clothes to dry in the late afternoon August sun. Flowers grew along a fence; yellow, orange, and lilac. A vegetable garden was near to harvesting. It was so domestic, so much like a real home again. He spoke again without turning around.

"I never believed that I would ever tell another soul as long as I lived that I loved them. Never. I just didn't think it possible. But…I love you. I haven't been able to do much of anything since you left, dammit…because I love you. And everything in my life was suddenly different without you."

Adam's voice was low, deep, pained, and genuine. Eva could see very clearly the tension of his body, all across the taut broad shoulders and the stiff stance of his legs. Eva could feel his need, held in check until he'd said what he had to say.

Eva walked up behind him and stroked his arm and back in a familiar way. He turned his head with his ruggedly hewn features to look down at her. To anyone else he'd seem hard, closed, angry, unbending. But Eva knew better. "Was that so hard to say? That you love me?" she asked, awed. Adam's jaw tightened.

"I love you, Eva," he said slowly, distinctly. "And it was damned hard to say!"

Eva shook her head in confused wonder. "I wasn't sure you cared at all."

"I know. I did a hell of a job keeping it from you, didn't I?" he said bitterly.

"Yes, you did," Eva agreed softly, seeing some of his uncertainty and confusion. It was, however, very gratifying to know that Adam was as vulnerable as any man to doubts. Maybe in some ways, more so.

Adam suddenly laughed softly without any humor. "When I found you were gone, I said okay, the hell with you! But I wanted to break your neck! Then I wondered why. I thought that was it. I'd never see you again."

Eva stroked his back again. "I was sort of hoping you'd write."

"Where?" he stormed again, making her flinch. "I didn't even know where you lived! New York, New Jersey…somewhere up here! I had to call Diane to get your address!" he continued in exasperation.

Eva let him shout his frustrations out. She smiled warmly at him, her brown eyes alight. She came right up to Adam and curved her arms around and up his back, resting her head on his chest. Adam stood stunned for an instant before folding himself around her, crushing her to him.

"Eva…" he said thickly against her temple.

"Max…I love you, too. But, you don't know how hard it was, losing everything and starting over…"

"I think I do. I might have lost Diane, never really gotten to know her if it wasn't for you."

"I've done things and have been things in the last two years I never would have dreamed of when Kevin was alive."

"I know," he whispered, holding her.

"You used to tease me that I'd make a good lawyer. Well…I decided I think I'd like to try out for law school. I mean, I have a lot of other schooling to do first, but…I think I can do it!" She pulled back her head to look up into his now serious, attentive eyes. "When I was on St. John with you, I found out I could love again, too. And I fell in love with you…"

Adam's hands came up to gently cup her face. Very slowly the drawn look was leaving his face.

''With you I discovered another part of myself, another woman who was passionate, giving, and free. She loves you very much.''

Adam let out a barely audible sigh and bent to pull a kiss in a tender manner from her smiling lips. ''And what about the woman here and now?''

Eva smiled impishly, hugging him. ''She feels the same way. It's a package deal. If you take part of me, you have to take all!''

She was finally rewarded with a slow smile curving Adam's wide well-shaped mouth. He kissed her again, deeply and lingeringly, and didn't hear Eva's mother reenter the house. Embarrassed and worried about what her mother would think, Eva tried to pull away from Adam, but he wouldn't release her and continued to kiss her with thorough deliberation.

''My, my!'' Mrs. Stewart chuckled in amusement and continued through the house with an empty laundry basket.

Finally Adam lifted his head, but Eva was already beginning to feel light-headed and aroused. ''Do you think she'll mind?'' Adam asked huskily.

''I—I don't think so,'' Eva managed.

''Have you told her anything about me?''

''I told her everything.''

Adam arched a brow in doubt.

''Well…not everything. But she knows that I…''

His hands moved up from her waist to just under and to the sides of her breasts. Eva shivered with the sensual touch. Her arms curved around his upper arms. ''That you, what?'' Adam prompted seductively.

Eva looked up at him. ''That I love you,'' she whispered.

Adam raised a hand to touch her cheek, trail his fingers

down her smooth skin to her jaw. Eva rubbed her cheek against the large hand affectionately. His thumb brushed across her bottom lip. "I wish I'd known," Adam said lowly, but it was just a statement of fact and not meant as a criticism of her.

"I had to tell her, Max. You weren't here and I had to talk to someone. I kept thinking of Kevin and Gail when I got home. Suddenly I felt so guilty. St. John made everything seem so unreal. I wasn't sure anymore what had really happened."

Adam laughed in self-derision and shook his head slightly. "It was very real to me. Remind me to show you the hole I punched in the kitchen wall sometime, when I found out you were gone…"

Eva's mouth dropped open and her eyes widened. "You're kidding!"

He shook his head no. "And I threw some of my research books off the deck. I still can't find one of them," he said in a rueful voice.

Eva started to laugh at her mental image of an angry Adam Maxwell taking out his displeasure on anything close at hand. "Oh Max! I'm sorry!"

"You should be!" he growled roughly, amusement nonetheless shining from his eyes. Eva's smile slowly faded. She touched and stroked his arms again.

"Maxwell…I—I need to love you," she said struggling with her own knowledge. Adam looked at her tenderly, watching the lovely glow of her face, slipping his arms around her back, bringing her hips and chest against him.

"When…" he whispered thickly.

Eva felt a sudden rush of blood to her neck and face at his implication. She looked down at the muscle of his chest imprinted under the fabric of his shirt, his male nipple outlined. "That's not what I meant..." she responded softly.

Adam put a hand under her chin and lifted her face to his. "Eva...I know what you meant." And he gently gathered her against his chest again. He brushed a kiss on her forehead, down to her cheek. He squeezed her suddenly, bending to bite erotically on her earlobe, his hand searching down her back to her curved bottom.

Eva gasped softly and turned her head to kiss his throat, feeling her body start to tremble with the desire he was bringing to life within her. She was fast thinking that she needed to be closer to him. It was Adam who actually voiced both their desire and need.

"Can't we go somewhere to be alone?" he asked a little impatiently.

"Where are you staying?" Eva asked simply. Adam's brow cleared and he grinned wolfishly.

"See how bad I've gotten? How come I didn't think of that?" He released her completely. "Go tell your mother you're going to be very late for dinner."

"But...what reason should I give her?" Eva frowned, struggling for a conservative excuse that wouldn't shock her mother.

Adam put his hands on her shoulders. "If she knows you love me, Eva, I think she'll figure it out!" He turned her and pushed her gently toward the door through which her mother had recently disappeared.

"Maxwell?"

"Ummmmm?"

"How long are you going to stay here?"

The words were absorbed by the hair on Maxwell's chest. Eva lay half across his torso, one leg lying between his, the other leg pressed against his thigh. Maxwell's left arm was bent back behind his head and the right was around Eva, the large hand rhythmically stroking up and down her back, side, and thigh.

"How long do you want me to stay?"

Eva heard the question but did not answer. Her sense of caution was still in play. "I was just wondering about your research. The ship and the house…"

Maxwell sighed deeply, silently. "The experiments are under control. They'll wait for me. Troy has the ship…"

Now it was Eva's turn to sigh. She gently pulled away from Adam and climbed off the bed. She walked gracefully over to the low, long dresser, feeling in the dark until she located Adam's watch. The illuminated face read almost eight o'clock. She put it down feeling that it shouldn't be that late. Maxwell had only just arrived. Sometime soon she knew he'd have to leave. Knowing that they loved each other hadn't really settled anything.

Maxwell hoisted himself up against the headboard of the large bed, stuffing pillows behind his back. He watched the dark form of Eva as she stood across the room from him. He watched as she went to draw open the orange curtains of the hotel room, just enough to show the sky gradually darkening after sunset.

"I can only stay a week," he finally answered her question. He saw her nod her head.

Eva was chilly in the dark air-conditioned room, but she didn't immediately go back to the bed or start to dress. She was suddenly panic-stricken that she'd do something foolish like cling to Maxwell. It came out of an overwhelming sense of happiness that he'd come to her, confessed he loved her, had loved her here in this impersonal room. But she was afraid to recognize that it might not be enough.

"What will you do the whole week?" she asked softly.

Maxwell bent a knee, putting his foot flat on the tangled sheets, and crossed his arms behind his head. It bulged the muscles in his shoulders and upper arms. His eyes narrowed in her direction.

"I haven't worked it all out yet. The most important thing yesterday seemed to just get to you today," he whispered in his deep voice. He didn't like the distance she'd put between them again.

Eva turned to stare at him, lounging comfortably on the bed. They'd both been deliciously satisfied after having assuaged their immediate need. But she wondered if he'd considered afterward. She could see Adam clearly, but he couldn't really see her.

"What about Lavona?" Eva asked. Maxwell frowned deeply, his jaw tensing almost in anger. "You're not usually given to being foolish Eva...what's this about Lavona?"

Eva drew her arms up to her naked breasts. Her voice dropped with uncertainty. "I just—just thought that after I left..." Her voice trailed off.

"Dammit, Eva," Maxwell ground out suddenly. "You understood my relationship to Lavona as well as I did. You even told me so!"

But that was before Eva knew she loved him herself. Way before Lavona could ever be a threat to her.

"Don't forget you had what's-his-name after you. How was I supposed to feel?"

Eva looked up surprised. "How did you feel?" she whispered in curiosity.

"Damned jealous!" Maxwell said without hesitation. "I didn't like him anywhere near you!"

"But it wasn't the same thing! Everyone on St. John seemed to know about you and Lavona. There was absolutely nothing between me and Deacon!"

Maxwell grunted. His arms came down, one resting on his bent knee. "But I still didn't like it!"

Eva was amazed. "You have a lot of nerve!" she said, in a combination of true amusement and exasperation.

"I know," Maxwell said, completely unabashed. But his expression suddenly got very thoughtful. His brows furrowed together, as he began to understand her continuing doubts. "Look, Eva…Lavona is every man's fantasy of whom he'd most like to be with on an island. But I never intended staying forever on an island."

Eva swallowed hard trying not to yell out her real fears. She turned her back to him. "Anyway…there's your work…"

Maxwell quickly swung off the bed and stood up.

"And your daughter."

He took his time walking up to her, reaching out his hands.

"I'm thinking about school. I told my mother I want to find my own pla…"

Maxwell grabbed her and turned Eva roughly into his arms. He crushed her to him. Eva's face was pressed tightly to his chest.

"Oh, Maxwell…what are we going to do?" she asked in a broken voice.

Maxwell caressed her chilled flesh, warming her against his hard body. "We're going to sit and talk. We're going to work this out." He pushed her back to see her face, see tears glistening and threatening to spill from her eyes. He bent to her, his tongue brushing to coax her lips apart so he could kiss her with intimate meaning. He kept pulling and playing gently until Eva was soft and warm and calmer. Then he released her, turning her toward the bed. He sat on the edge pulling Eva down beside him.

"Eva…the first thing I wanted to do was see you. I wanted you to know that I loved you. The next thing I'm going to do is get reassigned to a research project in the States…"

"But you like doing research in the Virgin Islands!" Eva protested in his behalf.

"That's right, I do…" Maxwell took hold of her face and looked full into her eyes. "But they don't have law schools in the Virgin Islands."

Eva's eyes grew bright and wide. But she was still unsure of his meaning.

"What do you think of Washington, D.C.?" Adam asked her now, letting go of her face.

"I don't know. I've never been to Washington," Eva admitted.

"I could do a lot in Washington. I could go back with the Navy, or teach, or work for Smithsonian. You could go to Georgetown or to Howard University to study. But we'd be together."

"Max!" Eva breathed out, feeling joyous.

"I have a friend who works in the Defense Department who could help us find an apartment or a house. Something big…so Diane could visit…"

Eva went cold. She didn't think it a good idea that Diane be made aware of her arrangement with her father. But, of course, Maxwell would want to see his daughter now, as much as possible. "I—I don't know if we should…" Eva hesitated.

Maxwell frowned at her for a long moment. "What do you think I'm suggesting?" he asked in a tight voice.

"That we—we live together. I—I don't mind that. But you can't expect Diane…"

"I'm not saying we should just live together," he said

patiently, but his jaw tensed again, and he sighed. "Sometimes I'd like to shake you…"

"I don't know what to expect from you, Maxwell. Just because you say you love me doesn't make everything automatically clear," Eva said softly in self-defense.

Maxwell looked at her carefully and smiled wryly. "You're right." He stroked a hand up her arm to her shoulder to her neck. He began to massage there sensuously. His light brown eyes commanded her attention.

"I realize that you loved your husband very much. You were both very lucky. I believed you when you said you didn't necessarily want to marry again. I wasn't so lucky, and I knew for sure I didn't want to…"

Eva laced her fingers together and looked down at them resting on her bare thighs. Maxwell continued to gently rub her neck. His voice grew low and seductive.

"But you're not the kind of woman a man just sleeps with. If we do this…if I get a job in Washington and you get accepted to law school, then we should get married…"

Eva looked at him with so much love that Maxwell gulped a tight knot in his throat. He opened his arms and Eva fell into them against his chest. "I love you," he whispered. "And I need you!" They stayed that way a long time.

"It might take a while to work out everything. All my research stuff has to be shipped from St. John. The department may want to send someone else there in my place."

"Do you think you'll ever go back?"

"*We'll* go back. The house belongs to me," Adam informed her with a grin.

"And I suppose you have Diane's permission to marry me?" Eva teased.

Maxwell laughed shortly. "As a matter of fact, I do. But if I didn't, it wouldn't make any difference. I don't intend to let you go!" He pushed her away gently. "Eva…will you mind that she's not…"

Eva shook her head vigorously, dealing quickly with flashing images of Gail. "It's enough that Diane's yours. She'll be ours, and I'll love her, too." She looked shyly at him now. "And—and maybe later…"

"Yes…later," Maxwell crooned. He lowered his head and captured her mouth. He rocked his mouth hungrily back and forth over Eva's, drawing love and warmth from her and into himself. He went over on his side of the mattress, bringing her with him. Eva returned his embrace, sure now of so many things.

Maxwell worked a hand between them to caress and knead her breast, bringing the soft round button to a stiff peak. Eva pressed even closer to him. He placed her on her back and began to kiss her throat and neck. His mouth moved to her breasts, kissing over them, under them to her rib cage. His tongue played in the hollow of her navel.

"Max—Max!" she moaned and squirmed. "We—we have to go back to the house! My mother…dinner…" Her voice stopped as his hands slid featherlike along her thighs. He lifted his head.

"We? Is she expecting me back?"

Eva was voiceless. All of her feelings and attention had dropped below her waist. She forced herself to roll away from Maxwell. He caught and held her by the waist. Eva's head went back on the pillow as Maxwell's weight pinned her legs.

"You'll stay with us for the week…"

"But I have to go to Washington for a day and start work on arrangements. And I'm hoping to see Diane…"

"That's okay. But my mother would never forgive me if I let you stay at a hotel. She thinks I'm crazy as it is for leaving you in St. John."

"Smart woman," he murmured, finally letting her get up. Eva went to retrieve her undergarments, while Adam propped his head in his hand. He watched with appreciation as she wiggled into a pair of blue panties. She sat on the edge of the bed to pull on panty hose. Adam ran a finger down the center line of her brown back.

"Do I get to share your room?" he asked thickly, teasing her.

Eva laughed softly. "I don't think that's what Mom has in mind. There's another bedroom. It used to belong to my two brothers."

Maxwell slid a hand around her to a softly jutting breast. "How far is this room from yours?"

Eva pushed his roaming hand away. "It's right next to it. But for a week you can sleep alone!"

"Don't bet on it!" Adam growled, hooking her waist and pulling her unceremoniously back on the bed. He pulled off her partially donned hose, and her panties quickly followed.

"Maxwell!" Eva protested, starting a half-hearted struggle with him. Maxwell started to tickle her. Eva began to twist and laugh helplessly. When all resistance was out of her, Maxwell closed his arms around her and began to administer a number of searing kisses, his tongue probing deep inside her mouth. When she began to tremble again, it was for another reason.

He freed a hand to caress her thigh and all along the inside to her flowering center. He moved to lie over her and press his hips and hard middle suggestively against her. Eva's breathing became shallow and labored. Maxwell lifted his head.

"On second thought, maybe we should go have dinner with your mother."

"Max..." Eva pleaded, putting her arms around his neck and pulling him back to her quivering, ready body.

If you enjoyed what you just read,
then we've got an offer you can't resist!

Take 2 bestselling love stories FREE!

Plus get a FREE surprise gift!

Clip this page and mail it to Harlequin Reader Service®

IN U.S.A.	**IN CANADA**
3010 Walden Ave.	P.O. Box 609
P.O. Box 1867	Fort Erie, Ontario
Buffalo, N.Y. 14240-1867	L2A 5X3

YES! Please send me 2 free Harlequin Romance® novels and my free surprise gift. After receiving them, if I don't wish to receive anymore, I can return the shipping statement marked cancel. If I don't cancel, I will receive 6 brand-new novels every month, before they're available in stores! In the U.S.A., bill me at the bargain price of $3.57 plus 25¢ shipping & handling per book and applicable sales tax, if any*. In Canada, bill me at the bargain price of $4.05 plus 25¢ shipping & handling per book and applicable taxes**. That's the complete price and a savings of 10% off the cover prices—what a great deal! I understand that accepting the 2 free books and gift places me under no obligation ever to buy any books. I can always return a shipment and cancel at any time. Even if I never buy another book from Harlequin, the 2 free books and gift are mine to keep forever.

186 HDN DZ72
386 HDN DZ73

Name	(PLEASE PRINT)
Address	Apt.#
City	State/Prov.	Zip/Postal Code

Not valid to current Harlequin Romance® subscribers.
Want to try another series? Call 1-800-873-8635
or visit www.morefreebooks.com.

* Terms and prices subject to change without notice. Sales tax applicable in N.Y.
** Canadian residents will be charged applicable provincial taxes and GST.
   All orders subject to approval. Offer limited to one per household.
   ® are registered trademarks owned and used by the trademark owner and or its licensee.

HROM04R

©2004 Harlequin Enterprises Limited

Silhouette Desire

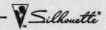

SPECIAL EDITION™

THE **COWBOYS** OF **COLD CREEK**

Love on the ranch!

NEW FROM
RaeAnne Thayne

DANCING IN THE MOONLIGHT
May 2006

U.S. Army Reserves nurse Magdalena Cruz
returned to her family's Cold Creek ranch from
Afghanistan, broken in body and spirit. Now
it was up to physician Jake Dalton to work his
healing magic on her heart....

Read more about the dashing Dalton men:
Light the Stars, April 2006
Dalton's Undoing, June 2006

There comes a time in every woman's life when she needs more.

Sometimes finding what you want means leaving everything you love. Big-hearted, warm and funny, Flying Lessons is a story of love and courage as Beth Holt Martin sets out to change her life and her marriage, for better or for worse.

Flying Lessons

by

Peggy Webb

Available May 2006
TheNextNovel.com

HN42